Tomorrow and Yesterday

Between the Lines Publishing

Published by Between the Lines Publishing (USA) as Willow River Press (imprint)
410 Caribou Trail, Lutsen, Minnesota 55612, USA

www.btwnthelines.com

Cover artist: Jim Tetlow

Tomorrow and Yesterday
Kris Francoeur

Paperback ISBN: 978-1-950502-19-6

For Sam – who always believed that I would be a published author, and who continues to motivate me as a writer and as a human being.

For Paul – who shows love, compassion, acceptance, humility, and unfathomable courage every single day. I can write about true love because he taught me what it is.

Prologue

The air was so cold, it was hard for her to breathe. Who was she kidding? It could have been a balmy, sunny day, and she still would have felt the clogging tightness of her throat, air barely able to get through to her lungs. So the biting late November air really didn't matter. The small shards of ice pelleting her face as the storm rolled in didn't matter either. Neither did the painful cold that was seeping through her jeans from sitting on the stone wall. Her voice trembled. "I don't even know if you'd still like chocolate or not." She looked at the sky, so dark and foreboding. "I wish we could have had the time to get to know each other as adults, Jake."

She sat on the seawall for a long time, looking out at the gray, raging ocean, her heart aching for what could have and should have been. With trembling gloved hands, she pulled the cupcake wrapper off the pastry, stuffing it in her pocket without caring if she dirtied her puffer coat. With tears running down her cheeks, she bit one half of the small pastry, swallowing the chocolate cake with vanilla frosting without really tasting it, or allowing herself any joy from the decadent confection. Then, with an angry motion, she threw the rest of the cupcake out into the ocean, seeing it bob on the waves for just a moment before it sank. "Happy birthday, Jakie. I love you and miss you."

Tomorrow and Yesterday

Chapter One

Three months later, Delaney hugged her cousin one more time. "Go, that's the final call for your flight. Have a great trip, and love you."

He nudged her arm. "You could still come with us, you know. Hawaii would do you a world of good."

"Nah. You know me, I don't know what to do with myself when I'm not working. I'd make you all crazy."

"No, you wouldn't. C'mon, Del, go with us." He tried to think of a way to convince her, "Do something spontaneous for once! Just get a ticket and join us. I'll buy the mai-tais. Come with us!"

"Not this time. You go have fun." She shrugged. "Besides, I'll get home late tonight, and will get a couple hours sleep before work tomorrow."

"Seriously, you need to start taking a break once in a while."

She'd heard that so many times before. "Yeah, yeah, yeah."

Delaney sat at the gate for her flight—people watching and knitting—with one wireless earbud in, listening to a podcast about the use of mindfulness in modifying the behavior of young children. The space was cold, so she wrapped her scarf around her neck and up over the side of her head with the earbud.

Just then, an airline attendant came to the nearby desk. Delaney watched as a tall, dark-haired man strode up to the desk, clearly agitated. "Excuse me, I'm booked on a flight to San Francisco, but I just got a call about a family emergency, and I need to get back to Boston as quickly as possible. Can I get on this flight?"

The woman looked at her computer screen. "I'm sorry, sir. This flight is fully booked, and everyone has already been checked in, so I don't have any options."

His voice was sharper than he expected. "My brother and his wife just gave birth to their daughter, and she was born almost three months early, and is in intensive care. I need to get back home!"

Calmly, the woman said, "Sir, have a seat for a moment. Let me see if there is anything I can do."

"Thank you." James sat down at the end of the seat row nearest to the desk, willing himself to control his agitation.

While the attendant was on the phone and looking at her computer, James noticed a young woman sitting off to the side, knitting. Always on the lookout for interesting visuals, James noted the shades of gray with her. Black boots rested on a black carry-on. Charcoal gray leggings led to a medium-gray tunic sweater, a light gray scarf wrapped around her neck, and white-blonde ringlet curls were visible sticking out from under the scarf. The oddity of the picture was the painfully bright scarf she was knitting, creating the image of a rainbow cascading down over the grays and blacks. James wished he could take a few minutes to sketch the scene, but instead tried to commit it to his memory so he could sketch it later

Just then, the attendant cleared her throat, wanting his attention. James jumped up and strode over to the desk. He sounded hopeful. "Am I on the flight?"

"No, sir. I looked at all the options." Her affect didn't change. "I am truly sorry for your family situation, sir, but I can't do anything about it."

Desperation filled him. "Can't you do an 'all call' to see if someone would be willing to take a later flight?"

"I can only do that when the airline has oversold the flight. That's not the case here." She smiled calmly, used to unhappy passengers. "I'm sorry, sir, but I can't help you."

"There has to be a way!"

"There isn't." She stopped smiling. "I need to ask that you step away from the counter, please."

Delaney had watched the whole encounter with interest, feeling for his distress. As the man stepped back, she saw the look of pain and frustration on his face, and her soft heart clenched tightly. For a moment, she allowed herself to recognize how attractive he was, but stuffed that aside.

As he walked away from the desk, she saw him pull a cell phone from his pocket, and seconds later she heard him say, "Mom, I can't get there until tomorrow morning. The last flight to Boston is full."

Making a quick decision, Delaney stood up and walked to the desk. "Excuse me."

The attendant looked up from her screen. "Yes?"

"If I wanted to give that man my seat, could I?"

The woman's eyes widened. "Yes, I guess you could. I would need to void your ticket, then issue him one in its place."

Delaney slid her boarding pass over the counter. "Do it."

"You don't need to go to Boston?"

"I do. But I can wait until the morning flight. He can't."

"You understand that you'll still need to pay for your flight, so really, you'll be paying for two flights?"

"I know, it's fine." Delaney walked away from the desk, having been booked on the early morning flight to Boston. She could go to a hotel, or instead, she could just stay in the airport. As she contemplated the options, the attendant called her name. "Ms. Adams?"

Delaney turned back to look at the woman. "Yes?"

The woman motioned her over and lowered her voice. "You know I couldn't comp your flight for you, and I'm sorry about that because you were being really kind. But I can give you a pass to the airline's club, and I've reserved a room there for you so you can get a little sleep."

Delaney was touched, and her face showed it. "Thank you. I really appreciate it."

"My pleasure." She tipped her head slightly, smiling. "It's nice to see someone being kind to a stranger. Thanks for reminding me of the goodness of people."

Delaney gathered her bags as the attendant picked up the microphone. "This is United Airlines, paging the passenger who needs to get to Boston tonight for family reasons. Please report to gate 28B as soon as possible."

Sitting at the concourse bar several gates down, James heard the announcement, and leaving a hefty tip on the counter, he almost sprinted to the gate.

The attendant looked up at him and smiled. "I have a seat for you, if you'd still like it."

"Yes, please!" As he handed over his credit card, he looked at her quizzically. "How'd that happen?"

She gestured down the concourse. "See the woman with the black bag?"

James looked and saw the young woman he'd noticed before. "Her? She was sitting over there."

"Yes. I guess she heard you, so she came over and gave up her seat."

"Really? Why'd she do that?"

"She said she could wait to get to Boston, and that you couldn't."

"Wow."

Tomorrow and Yesterday

Chapter Two

It had been over eighteen months since that flight and today Delaney tried to focus on the job at hand as she parallel parked on the busy street. That didn't stop her friend from continuing to talk. In vain, she tried to hold back her irritated tone. "Pam, for God's sake, I said I'd go with you. What more do you want?"

Her friend looked over at her and rolled her eyes, which Delaney caught in her peripheral vision. "Laney, we're going to an art opening, and James McDaniels is the hottest man on the friggin' planet. You're acting like we're going to a funeral!"

"I'm not here for fun, you are!" Laney tried to soften her voice. "You asked me to be your wingman, remember. I'm not here to meet anyone, just to keep you company until you get his attention. Seriously…" She turned off the ignition, and turned to look at Pam, seeing her friend's striking red hair against her dark green sundress which left nothing to the imagination. Next to Pam, Delaney felt plain and a little frumpy, something that didn't happen all that often. "You don't need me to help you get attention from men, never have, never will. You'd have been just fine without me." She nudged her friend's arm. "Let's face it, Pammy, you wanted me to drive so you can drink more than just a glass of wine, and without me, you'd have to be your own designated driver or call Uber."

Pam shook her head. "That's not the only reason. We haven't seen each other in weeks!"

"And we won't here. You're scoping out a man, I'm here to see art I don't care about and probably won't like!"

"His art is amazing!"

Delaney snorted. "As if you give a flying fuck about his art. You're here for his body, not his paintings."

"Fine! Just come on, Laney. Stop sulking and go with me. I want to be right on time, not too early, not too late." Pam looked at the sleek gold watch on her tan arm. "Let's hurry." She checked her makeup one more time in the mirror. "How do I look?"

"Like a goddess, like always." For the more than ten years since they'd met on the first day of college, Pam had been her closest female friend. When Delaney had decided to stay in Rhode Island after college and grad school, she'd been thrilled when Pam decided to stay as well. While they now lived more than a half hour apart, it still meant that they could see each other at least once a month. "Come on, let's get this over with."

At the gallery, Delaney was surprised to see the crowd was quite large. "Wow. I didn't expect this many people."

"Laneeeeey, how many times do I have to tell you? His work is the biggest thing on the art scene right now!"

"Big whup."

Pam stopped short, her eyes glittering. "Stop being a bitch. If you really don't want to go, then just go home. I'll Uber." She grinned, supremely confident of her own appeal. "Or maybe he'll give me a ride home."

"How are you so certain that he's single?"

Pam twisted one strand of Delaney's short blonde ringlet curls back into place. "Love the haircut, by the way."

Delaney had cut off her long hair the week before, donating it to charity, and now her short bob barely covered her ears. "Thanks. So?"

"Silly, I checked. My agent is friends with his agent." (Pam was a successful news anchor in Boston.) "I had her do some digging for me. Single, never married, lives alone on the shore out near Warwick, big oceanfront house with his studio."

Delaney raised one eyebrow. "Did you get his measurements too, or just the square footage of the house?"

"Both." Pam giggled. "Yum, yum, yum." She leaned forward to touch her forehead to Delaney's. "Come on, Laney, please come be my wingman."

Pam's begging always worked, and Delaney could feel her resolve weakening. "Fine."

In the gallery, Pam soon stopped to talk to several people she knew, so Delaney wandered further into the exhibit, slowly sipping a glass of champagne. The canvases ranged in size from no larger than a piece of notebook paper to giant ones covering whole walls. Not a huge lover of modern art, Delaney had to admit that there was something to this artist's talent. Even as blasé as she was about being there, the pieces still appealed to her emotionally.

As she stopped to gaze at one that caught her interest fully, she realized that she was in the line of traffic. Moving out of the way, she backed herself almost to the wall behind her, glad that small piece of space didn't have any art on it that she was blocking.

Standing there, she gazed at the sweeping lines and muted colors that gave her the sense of being on a bluff at sunset, gazing at the rolling ocean, feeling safe and loved. Delaney gave her head a sharp shake. How did a painting make her feel safe and loved? It must be the champagne. Still, she stood staring at the painting, letting herself be pulled into the emotions again. It felt like coming home.

Home? When was the last time she'd felt truly like she'd come home emotionally? Had she ever felt safe before she'd moved to Rhode Island? Maybe when she'd gone to her grandparents' house…

Closing her eyes, Delaney forced her brain to stop the train of thought. Nothing ever was gained by dwelling in memories. Focus on the painting!

Chapter Three

James McDaniels stood in the center of the main room of the gallery, trying to hide his irritation. How many more hours of this did he have to endure? He loved painting, loved hearing what people thought of his work, but he absolutely *hated* being the center of attention, or listening to the inane conversations going on around him. And the women! James certainly loved women, but groupies had never been his style. Meeting women at a gallery opening often meant that they were there because of his looks or his money, not for who he was as a person, let alone as an artist.

"Stop scowling." His mother's voice broke into his train of thought.

"I'm not scowling." He grinned innocently at his mother. "I'm thinking."

"No, you are standing there contemplating how much you hate these things, just like you used to hate the social events at the firm." She reached up to straighten his tie. "You are one of the warmest people I know, but you're *awful* in forced social situations." She smiled with understanding. "Just like me."

He laughed. "True." He gestured toward his brothers and father who stood on the other side of the room, chatting happily with anyone who came near them. "They always like this garbage, not us."

"I know." His mother squeezed his arm. "Go wander to the other rooms. They're less crowded, and you might be able to avoid people for a while."

"Good plan."

With a glass of straight scotch in hand, James walked through the large gallery, still pleased with the way his art was displayed. He hated events but loved seeing so many of his canvases shown in such perfect lighting.

His favorite painting of this show was in the farthest room of the gallery. Clearly the gallery owner didn't share his love of that particular work. Probably no one would be there, so he could sneak a couple minutes of relative quiet.

Rounding the corner, he found a woman standing alone, her back almost touching the wall across from the painting. Her blonde hair was cut short in a bob, and the ringlet curls looked so very touchable. One soft curl reached down to caress her cheek, and the urge to sweep it back from her face almost overcame him. Focusing on not touching her, he noticed how her sleeveless navy-blue dress, with the draped neckline, showed gorgeous curves, her bare legs leading down to spike-heeled sandals. Who the hell was she? Why was she standing here alone? He couldn't help himself from hoping that a boyfriend or husband wasn't about to come around the corner too. His mind still racing, he had the thought that no man would be stupid enough to let a woman like her wander off alone.

He walked toward her quietly, realizing that she was so engrossed in the painting that she hadn't seen or heard him approaching. He slowed a bit, not wanting to scare her. "Hi."

She turned to look at him, clearly startled. "Hi."

"What do you think of it?"

"Of what?" Delaney found herself feeling stupid as she looked at the man standing near her, recognizing him almost immediately. He was the man from the airport! The man that she'd dreamed of on and off since that moment she'd first seen his face caught in agitation. She realized that even in her heels, he was much taller than she was, his black hair sweeping back, almost reaching the collar of his gray blazer—the crisp white of the shirt showing off his tan. He was gorgeous, just as gorgeous as he was in her dreams. Delaney gave her head a small shake; she didn't think about men anymore. Period. Yup, she'd had some rather hot dreams about him, but now she was going to get out of here fast. She didn't date, didn't allow herself the luxury of a man in her head or in her bed. That was Pam's thing.

Where was Pam? Couldn't Pam just meet the damn artist and let them go home? Then Delaney realized he had asked her something, and she had no idea what he was talking about. "I'm sorry, I wasn't concentrating. What was the question?"

"What do you think of the painting?" He gestured toward the canvas, and Delaney tried to refocus.

"I love this one." She tried to stand straighter, trying to make herself look more assured, thankful that there was no way he could know they'd crossed paths before. "I like some of the others, but this one has the greatest depth of emotion in it. It truly feels like love to me. If I was the artist, I would've insisted on this one being in the *front* gallery, not hidden back here."

Just then Delaney could hear high heels clicking on the floor, and she was shocked when she recognized the woman who appeared around the corner. "Gail?" she called more loudly than expected.

The older woman beamed as she stepped forward to wrap Delaney in a tight hug. "Delaney! So good to see you."

"You too."

Gail stepped back, seeing the look on James' face. "Delaney, I didn't know you'd met my son."

Delaney was shocked as she looked from the gorgeous man to the older woman. "Your son?"

"James McDaniels is my son, one of my sons, actually." She turned to him. "James, this is my friend and colleague, Delaney Adams."

Delaney looked up at the man in shock and horror. "You're James McDaniels? The artist?"

He grinned, suddenly enjoying how uncomfortable she looked. He held out his hand, forcing her to shake it. "I am. Nice to meet you."

She looked down at their hands for a second before pulling hers back. "I am so, so sorry. I was really out of line to say what I did about the placement of this painting."

He shook his head, still smiling. "I agree with you totally. Out of my works here, this is my favorite, but the gallery owner doesn't agree with us."

"Oh." Delaney looked around for someplace to put her glass, needing to get out of the awkward situation as soon as possible. "Anyway. Nice to meet you." She looked at Gail. "I'll see you next week."

Pam appeared by her side before she could escape. "Laney! There you are." She realized who was standing next to Delaney, and her voice dropped to almost a purr as she held out one perfectly manicured hand. "You must be James. Pam Needham."

Delaney's stomach rolled in distress, but she dutifully murmured, "Pam's the anchor of Boston 5 News."

James shook Pam's hand, wishing that both Pam and his mother would disappear and let him get back to the fascinating woman who was clearly trying to get away from him as fast as possible. "Pleasure to meet you."

Pam moved closer. "The pleasure is mine."

Just then the waiter showed up, and Delaney almost jumped to put the glass on the tray. "Pam, I have to take care of something at work. I need to go."

Pam didn't care. "I'll get a ride home."

Delaney looked at the two others. "Nice to meet you, James. Gail, see you soon."

And she left without sparing a look back, not waiting to see if anyone said anything to her.

Tomorrow and Yesterday

Chapter Four

At home that night, Delaney slipped out of the dress, and stepped into her favorite leggings and a faded Brown University t-shirt. What the hell had she been doing at the exhibit? Pam didn't need her help—or anyone's help for that matter—to attract a man. Never had, never would. And Delaney didn't need to be thinking about any man, ever again. Never. Never, never, never. She'd tried that before, and her marriage had been a total disaster. Now it was time to just focus on her work, period. She couldn't let herself think about the tall gorgeous man with those deep, dark eyes. Eyes that had looked at her so intently, like he actually cared about her opinion. She shook her head so sharply that for a moment she felt a touch of vertigo. Nope. *Stop it.* It didn't matter that she'd seen him before Pam, back so long ago in Chicago. Or that he'd made her heart flutter just seeing him then, and again tonight. The man was probably naked in bed with Pam by now.

With a sigh, Delaney sat down cross-legged on her bed, pulling her laptop over and hitting the power button. She wouldn't think about the flash of jealousy she felt at the idea of Pam in bed with James. She *wouldn't*. She'd gone to the gallery to help Pam meet him; that was the plan, and it had worked. It didn't matter if Delaney found him attractive. She didn't date, Pam wanted him, and she'd never be the type of friend to poach someone else's man. Shit, never mind.

An hour later, Delaney shut her laptop, glad she'd cleaned up the emails from work. At least she could start her Saturday with a relatively clean slate. Maybe she'd go for a hike on the Cliff Walk all by herself.

After watching a bit of TV, she reached over to turn off the light, just as her phone lit up with a text.

Delaney grimaced as she saw it was Pam. Did she really have to read a text this late at night about how good James was in bed? Delaney reached for the phone, knowing damn well that if she didn't respond, Pam would keep texting.

It was short. *J wasn't as interesting (or interested) as I thought he would be, but his older brother, Thomas, wow, wow, wow. We are meeting for lunch tomorrow...*

Delaney squashed down the rush of relief. At least she didn't have to deal with Pam being with James! She typed, *Congrats! Have fun–night.*

Night, Laney—love you.

Later, Delaney awoke covered in cold sweat, her heart pounding. Would the nightmares never stop? Lately they had been less frequent, but still happened fairly often. How long would she have to relive that night? Were dreams of that hell the only way she could see Jake and her mother in her mind? In the light of day, she could barely remember what they looked like, but at night, the images were so vivid...

Turning on the light, she reached for the novel that was always on her nightstand. Those nightmares were part of the reason she needed to keep her life simple. For the few short years of her marriage, she'd been able to justify them to Tom, but that sort of secrecy was too much for her now. Keep it simple, stupid, that was her motto. Right?

Tomorrow and Yesterday

Chapter Five

Gail McDaniels grinned as she heard her son's voice in the hallway. She shouted, "Morning, Jimmy."

He came into the kitchen, seeing both of his parents sitting at the breakfast table, croissants and coffee in front of them as usual. For a split second he wondered if he'd ever seen them have something else for breakfast. "Morning Mom, Dad."

She gestured toward the coffee pot. "Help yourself."

He poured a mug, adding a splash of cream. "Thanks."

He joined them at the table. After a few minutes of small talk about the event the night before, Gail looked searchingly at her son. "You want to know how to contact her?"

He tried to look innocent. "Who?"

"Don't 'who' me, you ass. Delaney. Delaney Adams. You want to know how to contact her."

Damn his mother for always being a step ahead of him! He rolled his eyes at his father who was trying to hold back a laugh. "Yes, damn it. I thought I had her name right after you introduced us, but I can't find any contact information at all."

His father chuckled. "I thought that redhead had you all sewn up."

"*Hell, no*. She was so subtle it made my teeth hurt."

His father looked confused. "What do you mean?"

"I mean I knew who she was the moment she introduced herself. She had her agent talk to Ginny, who gave me a heads up before the opening." He shook his head. "Seriously, she used our *agents*? So romantic!." He looked hopefully at his mom. "So, you going to help me or not?"

She took a sip of her coffee, seeing her middle son looking more interested in a woman than she'd seen him in years. For a while, she'd been afraid he'd never meet his soul mate. Maybe Delaney was the one for him. "Here's the thing, sweetie. I can give you her work contact information, but, even though I've known her professionally for several years now, I don't have any other information." She grimaced. "She's a closed book about anything other than her job."

Knowing how friendly his mom was, this surprised him. "What do you mean?"

"I mean, she's the most dedicated professional I know, and she is fabulous to work with, but she's very clear that her personal life is private, period." She looked uncomfortable. "I tried to get her to come to Fourth of July two years ago, thinking that she might be a good match for Tony, and she turned me down flat. She calmly thanked me for the invitation and said that she didn't do social things like that."

"You tried to set her up with Tony?" James' voice rose louder than he'd intended, suddenly furious at the thought of this woman being with his older brother.

Gail had raised five sons, so one of them almost shouting didn't rattle her. "Yes, I did. You were with Nicole then. Delaney is smart, motivated, and beautiful. Why wouldn't I try to set her up with your brother?"

Because I want her, damn it!"

Gail tried to hold back a laugh, not completely successfully. "Didn't know that then, peanut. Now, do you want my help or not?"

When James left his parents' house later, he had Delaney's work number tucked into his pocket.

Tomorrow and Yesterday

Chapter Six

On Monday, Delaney walked into her office, already rubbing her temple as her assistant followed her, giving her a list of issues to solve. "Yeah, Laney, beyond all that, Tito and Cindy are both out, and we don't have subs. What do you want to do?"

Delaney reviewed the possible solutions almost instantly. "Combine Tito's group with Lucy's, Cindy's with Ashley's and I will do the lunches and recesses."

"Got it." Alyssa, her ever-so-efficient assistant, handed her a slip of paper. "This message was on your line this morning. Sorry, Laney, if I'd known it was a personal message, I wouldn't have listened."

Delaney took the slip of paper. "No worries." She shoved the message slip into her pants' pocket, already forgetting about it, fully focused on the busy day ahead.

Back at home that night, Delaney tiredly dropped the takeout box of Thai noodles on the kitchen counter, then dumped her leather tote bags on a chair. Without breaking stride, she walked into her bedroom, pulling her blouse over her head, and slipping out of her slacks. She pulled on faded shorts and a tank top, glad that she'd remembered to turn on the air conditioning timer before she went to work that morning. The heat was supposed to continue all week, and already, Delaney was tired of being hot and sticky.

Gathering her dirty clothes, she grabbed the bathroom hamper, knowing she needed to throw in a load of laundry before eating her dinner.

At the washer, Laney slowly turned all the clothes right side out, checking pockets, knowing how often she left scraps of paper in them, causing a mess with her clothes.

When the small slip of paper fell from her pants, Laney immediately recognized it as a message slip. She put it on the top of the washer, finished sorting her clothes, and started the machine.

She walked back to the kitchen, put the slip of paper next to her dinner, poured a glass of cold white wine, and sat down at the counter. How many dinners had she eaten perched on a stool? With a sigh, she thought further, how many dinners had she eaten *alone*? She took a sip from her cup, then took a bite of the noodles that were now room temperature. Should she re-heat them? No, why bother? As she unfolded the paper, she tried to push aside the momentary awareness of how lonely she was.

Shock flowed through her as she read Alyssa's neat script: *James McDaniels called on Saturday afternoon.* Then Laney saw the quote marks, meaning that Alyssa had shifted to exact transcription. "*Delaney, we met at the gallery last night. I apologize for calling your work number, but I didn't know how else to reach you. I'd love to get together, maybe for a drink or coffee, to talk more. Give me a call at ...*"

For a split second, Delaney felt absolute pride and delight flood her. A man was more interested in *her* than Pam! Had that ever happened before? Not to her knowledge. *That* man was interested in her! Then the crushing weight of her own reality dried up the wave of pleasant emotions. She didn't date. Period. Too many questions. Too many nightmares that she couldn't explain to anyone. Too many ways to get into trouble.

Delaney ate another bite and stared at the message. James McDaniels wanted to go out with her? Seriously? The man was stunning. Breathtaking. Those dark eyes. The broad shoulders. The way his long fingers had felt when they shook hands. What would it be like to hold those hands? To have those fingers touch her face? To feel them unzip her dress? To have him do the things she'd seen him do in her dreams?

What the hell was she doing thinking about this guy unzipping her dress? She didn't need a man in her life! Damn it, she didn't!

So, what was she going to do about his message? Ignore it? Call him back and say no? God, no! She couldn't call him and say she didn't want to go out with him. It wasn't that she didn't want to—she couldn't! Normal people didn't have blank slates for their pasts, and even a casual date or two could lead to too many questions that she couldn't or wouldn't answer.

Thinking of how good he'd looked at that gallery, and the way he'd focused on her when they were alone, Delaney felt her stomach flutter. Wow! He'd asked *her* out. Not Pam, not someone else. *Her*. Delaney Adams had been asked out by James McDaniels! What if she just went out for coffee with him? Somewhere really public, just to be polite. After all, Gail was her colleague and friend. It wouldn't be right to offend her son. One coffee, in public, she'd pay for it, very casual like. Then thank him, leave, and not look back. One little coffee. Just one little coffee.

Delaney pushed away the half-eaten box of noodles, no longer hungry. She took a sip of the now tepid wine and looked at the message again. Coffee, one time, would be fine. She'd have the thrill of knowing someone like James was interested enough to call her, then go on with her life. No complications.

Should she call him? Text him? If she texted him from her cell, it would mean that he would have her private number. Did she want that? What if she called or messaged him from her work number instead? That would keep the firewall up. She could use the texting program she used for parents of students. The one where her number was shielded by he school number, but still was a text rather than a call. Then he could also text her back, and although he wouldn't have her number, it would go directly to her phone, not to her office number where Alyssa might pick up the message. That was a good plan!

Delaney stood up, gathering the box and utensils, putting the rest of her dinner in the fridge. Still trying to decide what to do, she then putthe few dishes in the dishwasher. Taking her glass of wine and her laptop to the living room—putting both on the coffee table—she turned on the Red Sox. It was already the seventh inning! She rubbed her temple, the slight headache pressing at her, as it often did when she was tired. She really needed to leave work earlier each day. She was paid to run a school, not live there. Yeah, right.

Sitting on the couch, she pulled the table closer so she could rest her feet on it. Her laptop open on her knees, she clicked the texting program, then slowly typed in his number. What should she say? Deliberately she typed, *Hi, it's Delaney. Thanks for your message. Sorry it took me so long to get back to you. I'd love to buy you a cup of coffee — how about Saturday at 9 at Sift?*

No. That sounded too formal and apologizing for taking so long to get back to him sounded too needy. She erased and started again. *Hi James, it's Delaney. Coffee sounds good. Sift at nine on Saturday?*

Too cold? Too brief? She edited to, *Hi James, it's Delaney. Coffee would be good. Saturday at Sift?*

She reread the message. That worked. Friendly but not too friendly. Just right. She hit send and closed the laptop. Leaning back against the cushions, she turned to the screen, smiling as Mookie Betts hit a homerun.

Not five minutes later, her phone lit up with a text. *My mom was right.*

His mom was right? What did that mean? She opened her laptop and typed, *What do you mean?*

She said you had a pretty tight control over your personal information — you sent a masked number text…

Hmm… Most people didn't know about such systems. *How do you know it's masked?*

I was/am a lawyer — used them all the time.

Well that was an interesting piece of information. A lawyer and artist. What an interesting combination. *Fine. I used a masked number. I'm still texting you, aren't I?*

Good point. Coffee at Sift sounds great, but you don't have any time between now and Saturday?

Delaney sat on the couch, trying to push down the little thrill when she read that last text. He wanted to see her before Saturday. That meant he was more than a little interested, right? She shook her head. Stop it! She needed to keep in mind that this was just a coffee. She needed to put on the brakes before anything more. *I go to work early; didn't think you were thinking a pre-dawn coffee.*

I don't care what time we meet. I'm up early, you pick the time, but how about tomorrow?

Shit! Tomorrow was so, so soon. Too soon. What would she wear? For a moment, she thought back to the really cute blouse she'd seen walking through Providence Place Mall on

Sunday afternoon. If she stopped there tomorrow after work, she could wear that to meet him on Wednesday. *I can't tomorrow but could Wednesday. 7:30 at Sift?*

How early do you need to be at work? I could meet at 7 if you want.

That would work. She would be up early, could go have coffee, and still be at work long before the kids arrived. *Sounds good.*

See you then.

Chapter Seven

The next afternoon, Alyssa came into Delaney's office. "Hey, Laney. I'm heading out. Need anything before I go?"

Laney looked up, surprised at how late it was. "No. All good." She paused. "I may be a few minutes late tomorrow."

"Going for coffee?" Alyssa grinned. "That man is spectacular!"

"How'd you know?"

"Laney, you got a message from a man asking you for coffee or a drink. I did the normal thing and googled him. The images tab had not only his art, but photos of him. Damn, honey! Good for you!"

"Just coffee. Nothing more. You know me, I'm too busy to date anyone."

"Bullshit. You need a life outside of here."

It was a familiar refrain. "Yeah, yeah. I know."

"See you tomorrow." Her eyes sparkled. "Take the whole day if you want, I'll take care of everything here."

At the mall, Delaney looked at herself in the mirror. The blouse—a soft swirl of pinks, purples and blues—complemented her blue eyes and blonde hair beautifully. It even made it look like she'd gotten some color this summer. The neckline dipped just low enough to show the swell of her breasts. With her favorite black skirt and flats, it would be a great outfit.

The next morning, Delaney stood in front of her bathroom mirror, twisting to see how she looked from all angles. Her legs looked long and tan, even though she was just over five feet tall. The blouse was perfect. She stood on tiptoe to get closer to the mirror, adding a tiny bit more mascara to her lashes.

At five minutes before seven, she pulled into a parking spot across the street from the popular bakery. Keeping her sunglasses on, she carefully clicked the lock on her remote before walking across the street, seeing James heading toward the bakery. Glad her eyes were hidden, she allowed herself to look him over head to toe. Dressed in blue-gray button-down shirt and dark-gray slacks, his eyes covered with aviator sunglasses, his dark hair glinting with the slightest of auburn highlights in the sun—he was gorgeous. *Gorgeous*. Just as gorgeous as he'd seemed to her the first time she saw him in the airport. Her body immediately responded to seeing him— her breathing quickening and her stomach feeling fluttery. *Get a grip!* she groused to herself.

Stopping on the sidewalk in front of the bakery, she waited for him to reach her. Her voice was breathier than she intended. "Hi."

He grinned down at her. "Hi."

She gestured toward the bakery. "Coffee? What would you like?"

"Let's go see what they have today."

Inside, they joined the line of customers inching forward. Feigning interest in the list of available pastries, Delaney avoided small talk until they reached the counter. She quickly ordered a coffee and an almond chocolate croissant before looking up at James. "What would you like?" she asked as she reached for her purse.

He covered her hand with his. "I've got this." He looked at the clerk. "The same, please."

Delaney shook her head. "No, I've got it." She looked around. "I'll get our order; you go find us a seat."

James wanted to argue but sensed that this was going to be a sticking point for her. "Inside or out?"

"Out." She gestured toward the back door. "The courtyard?"

"Perfect." He took a couple napkins. "See you out there."

As Delaney stepped out the back door with their breakfast, James let himself look at her as intently as he sensed she'd done earlier. The little black skirt swirled around her legs as she moved. For a woman so small, her legs looked impossibly long. Her blonde hair sparkled in the sunlight, making him itch to run his fingers through it. Was her hair as soft as it looked?

When she reached the small table, she put the coffee and pastry in front of him.

"Thank you."

"You're welcome." James watched in interest as she carefully crossed her legs, tucking her skirt so that it wouldn't move in the slight breeze. She took a sip of coffee—her eyes still covered by her glasses—and looked at him. "Good morning."

"Good morning." He grinned slightly wickedly, and Delaney could feel her pulse start to race again. "Thanks for getting up early to have breakfast with me."

"Likewise."

Making small talk with her was clearly not going to be easy. James was used to women gushing all over him, talking incessantly, and wanting his full attention. He got the sense that Delaney would be perfectly comfortable sitting in complete silence, and that if anything made her uneasy, it would be his scrutiny. A woman that attractive—and as professionally accomplished as his mother had said she was—was usually more relaxed in such situations. This was going to be interesting!

James took a sip of his coffee, then asked, "Okay, so now that I convinced you to meet me for coffee, who are you Delaney Adams, and how did you end up at my show last weekend?"

"Well, you know that I'm the director of Children's World, and," she paused, suddenly even more uncomfortable. "I went to the show because my friend Pam…" Her voice trailed off, not wanting to say that they'd gone because Pam wanted to jump him.

"Because your friend Pam was agent-stalking me?" His voice showed his humor.

Delaney was just pulling off her sunglasses as he said this, and her eyes widened in shock. "You knew?"

He laughed, glad to see her reaction. "I knew. My agent called to give me a heads-up earlier that day." He shrugged. "I met Pam, introduced her to my brother, and went on with my life." As a cloud passed over the sun, James too removed his sunglasses, and for the first time that morning, Delaney could see his dark-brown eyes. They were even more beautiful than she'd remembered: smoky-quartz irises framed by long lashes with the hint of laugh lines at the corners. "In fact, what I did was go bug my mother to give me your number."

She tried to hide her pleasure. "Which she did."

"Sort of. She said she only had your work number, which led me to leaving you that message on your office line. I've never done that before." Taking another sip, he laughed. "Thanks for the new experience."

Delaney held back a snicker. "The funny thing is that usually I get to the office before my assistant, so I check my own messages. On Monday, I had an early meeting, so Alyssa checked them, and got your message before me." She gave up trying to keep a straight face and giggled. "She was mortified, I was mortified, but when I said I might be late today, she gave me grief about going for coffee with you."

Her laugh delighted him. "Good to know I provided some amusement."

"Anyway, yes, I went to the show because Pam wanted to meet you." She wiped a crumb off her skirt. "Modern art isn't really my thing. I went to the show because of her, no offense."

"None taken." He leaned back in his chair, studying her intently. "And you liked one of my pieces a lot, but disliked the placement, and when your friend showed up, you disappeared like magic." He tipped his head. "Did you really have a work issue, or were you just trying to escape?"

Delaney reached up and twirled some strands of hair near her left ear. James would later realize it was a common gesture when she was uncomfortable. "Both. I always have work stuff to do, but after I made the comment to you about where I thought the painting should have been exhibited, I was embarrassed that I'd been so rude. Then when Pam showed up, I figured you'd be busy with her, so I took off."

"Did it bother you?"

Delaney was completely confused. "Did what bother me?"

"That you thought I'd be busy with Pam. Did that bother you at all?"

The look on her face was priceless as she clearly struggled with how to answer him. Regardless of what she said, James saw the flash in her eyes that revealed it had bothered her, maybe a lot.

She took a deep breath, sat up straighter, and looked directly at him, clearly understanding he was challenging her by asking such a blunt question. "Yes. It did."

The grin on his face was immediate. She rolled her eyes in irritation. "Happy now?"

"Yeah. I am." He took another sip. "Okay, now that we've settled that, tell me about your school. I know you collaborate with my mom, but that's about it."

They fell into easy conversation, chatting about her work while James watched in fascination as she relaxed. Their coffees had been drained and their pastries were nothing but crumbs by the time she looked at her watch in horror. "Shit! I didn't realize it was so late." She started to gather her dishes. "I apologize, James, I need to get to school."

"Don't apologize." He reached out and rested his hand on hers as she was picking up a spoon. "Delaney. Stop for a moment."

She froze, a blush creeping up her cheeks. "Yes?"

"Thank you for meeting me this morning." He grinned. "Since you bought breakfast, how about I buy you a drink?"

She looked down at her lap, trying to stop the immediate rush of excitement at the idea of going out with him again, coupled with the cold realization that dating anyone was a bad idea. Damn it! If only she could have just been plain Delaney Adams, nothing more. Her voice was tentative. "James…"

"Ouch. You're about to turn me down." He smiled, trying to keep his voice light. "You seemed to enjoy yourself. Why not go for a drink with me? I'm not proposing, just asking you for a drink."

She looked at where his hand still rested on hers and, without thinking, turned her hand over so that they were palm to palm, and she could feel the warmth from his hand. "I did have a good time, it's just…"

His voice was gentle. "It's just what?"

Her voice came out in a rush as she tried to explain, "I don't date. I work around the clock, and it's just easier if I don't get tangled up in a relationship."

"I wasn't asking you for a relationship, I'm asking you for a drink." He chuckled. "Or coffee again, or whatever. Just another casual get-together."

The idea of spending more time with him was so appealing that Delaney could feel her resolve weakening. "The rest of the week will be really busy."

"Okay."

"What if we messaged each other a bit this week, and if things calm down for me, I could let you know and maybe we could get a drink on Sunday afternoon."

It wasn't the answer he wanted. He wanted her to ditch work for the day and spend it with him, letting him get to know her. But it was better than her turning him down. "That works."

After they cleared the table, they walked back out to the sidewalk. Delaney gestured at her car. "That's me."

"I know." He looked down at her, fighting the urge to lean over and kiss her goodbye, knowing it was too soon for that. "Sunday afternoon."

She corrected him with, "If things calm down."

"Fine." He chuckled. "If things calm sooner than that, let me know."

"I will."

Chapter Eight

Delaney pushed back from her desk; glad the morning had been as calm as it had so far. All her staff had come to work, no major issues with students, or the aging building, and even the AC was working. So why was she so fidgety?

Alyssa came in through the door, a can of seltzer in her hand. "So?"

"So, what?"

"Text him!"

"What are you talking about?"

"You had a good time, right?"

"Yeah, I did." She blushed. "I really did."

"Then text him, dummy."

Delaney was shocked. "I just had coffee with him this morning. That would sound desperate."

"He asked you out again! Stop being stubborn and text him, just to say hi. Thank him, *something*." She looked at her boss searchingly. "You're not getting any younger, you know."

"Oh, shut up."

Just then, her computer buzzed, showing a message had come into the texting program. It was brief. *Was going to try to wait until at least this evening to text you, but I can't. Thanks for breakfast this morning.*

Seeing the smile on Delaney's face, Alyssa chuckled. "That him?"

"Yeah."

"What's it say?"

Delaney read her the text, trying to hide her delight.

Alyssa sighed happily. "Wow. That's a hell of a message."

"I know!" Delaney suddenly looked unsure of herself. "Lyssa, I don't do this, you know that. I don't date."

"You should, Laney. You're amazing, and you deserve to have someone in your life." She reached out to nudge Delaney. "Don't overthink this, just enjoy it. See where it goes."

Was Alyssa right? Could it be that simple? Just see what happened? That went against everything in Delaney's makeup, not to plan every single aspect of her life while protecting her privacy with almost religious zealotry. "Okay." She saw the skepticism on Alyssa's face, so she sat up straighter. "Seriously. Okay. An amazing man asked me out, I said yes. I'm not making life decisions right now, just going to have some fun."

"So, text him back!"

Laney pulled the laptop closer. "What do I say?"

Alyssa shook her head and grabbed the edge of the laptop, pulling it back. "First of all, Laney, if you are going out with him again, and he already knows where you work, stop using the texting program and just text him directly from your phone. If he wants to stalk you, he already has enough information."

"But…"

"But nothing. If it doesn't work out, and he starts bugging you via phone, just block him. That's all. It would be a huge step for him to see that you actually trust him enough to give him your number."

"I'll think about it."

Think was all Delaney did for the next two hours. All she could contemplate was how much she'd actually enjoyed their time together that morning. As she did her normal recess duties—supervised swimming lessons and served snacks—she thought about James. How he'd laughed at several things she'd said, his eyes lighting up. How his hand had felt when it covered hers. How she thought she'd felt a little frizzle of energy when she'd turned her hand over in his. How she'd liked it when he'd held the door for her, smiling down at her.

Walking back toward her office, Alyssa called out, "Did you do it?"

"Not yet!"

"Laney, don't be stupid. The guy texted you hours ago. He's going to think you're blowing him off."

I'm not blowing him off! I'm just not jumping immediately."

"You're an idiot."

An hour later, Laney looked at her phone, grimacing at her words. *Thanks for this morning, it was fun. Sorry, it's been really busy today.* Was that truthful? Yes, saying it was fun was truthful. Saying she was busy wasn't. Should she remove it? Slowly she deleted the last sentence, then added, *How's your day?* Then she hit send, put her phone face down on the desk, and left her office quickly. As she walked by Alyssa without breaking stride, she said, "Going for a walk-through. I don't have my phone, so page me if you need me."

Alyssa shook her head. "You're a pip, Laney. You texted him, didn't you?"

"Yes."

"And now you're flipping out, so you're leaving your phone here?"

Her voice showed her irritation. "Yes, fine, you're right!"

"Then go for a walk, leave your phone behind, and I'll shout if I need you. Do you want me to answer your phones if they ring?"

Delaney grinned. "Cell no, office, yes."

"Got it."

Delaney wandered the building for almost an hour, catching up with staff and students, and playing with the kids for a bit. Finally, she realized that she was being childish by staying away from her office because she didn't know how she felt about sending that text. Did she want him to have answered while she was wandering, or not? Did she want to start texting him this often, or just keep to the schedule of their next planned get-together? What did she want?

Delaney stopped by the large windows on the second floor, looking down at the playground below, the city spread out behind it, fading down the hill. This was her favorite viewpoint in the entire complex, one where she often stood and watched recess, or just looked at the city. What did she want with James? Was she just having a little flirtation, or could this be more? Did she want more?

She leaned against the deep windowsill, pressing her forehead to the cool glass. It had been years since Laney had thought of anything other than work or allowed herself to have more than a very limited social life. She might have a few hours with Pam once a month, an occasional event after work with colleagues, or a weekly dinner with the retired widower next door. That was it. So far, she'd gone out for coffee with James, and he'd asked her for a drink. That was a whole lot more social activity than she was used to. Was this what she wanted?

Suddenly she grinned. Yes, this *was* what she wanted. She hadn't been thinking that she wanted a man in her life, but yes, deep down, she had to admit that the first moment she'd seen James in the airport, she'd felt something. Knowing she'd never see him again; she'd let herself have the occasional daydream about the mystery man. Now, she'd actually met him, and he'd asked her out, and her heart raced just thinking about him. When she'd realized who he was, the disappointment had been so deep, knowing that Pam was after him. How could she compete with Pam, after all? But she had! James was more interested in her than Pam.

Just then, Delaney heard footsteps and jumped back from the window just in time for five-year-old Sofia to come around the corner. "Hi, Sofia."

"Hi! Whatcha doing?"

"Looking at the playground."

"Why?" The child's look clearly showed that was a silly idea.

"Because I was thinking."

"Oh." The child reached up to take Delaney's hand, which she often did. "Want me to walk you to your office?"

"I would love that."

Sophia didn't release Delaney's hand until the little girl was waving goodbye from her doorway. As she walked away, Alyssa looked at Delaney and shook her head in amusement. "Sofia had to bring you back? What, you couldn't find a closet to clean to avoid your office longer?"

"Bite me," Delaney groused as she walked back into her office.

"No calls, boss. Just a couple text messages came in on your phone."

Delaney tried to not grin. Sitting down at her desk, she made herself take a small sip of water before she turned her phone over. There were two new messages from James.

Wow, something strange just happened — a phone number popped up for you instead of the blocked one... Everything okay?

As someone known for her sarcasm, Delaney enjoyed his message. Then she scrolled to the second one. *My mother would say that I am too flip. So, I should have held that first message back and just said it was good to hear from you. My day is good — yours?*

Looking at the time stamps, she knew both messages had come within minutes of sending hers. It was now over an hour later. She typed, *So far it's been a good day. Busy, sticky, but good.*

Sticky?

She laughed at his immediate response. *Sticky — I hang out with little kids. In this heat, they are sticky.*

Ahhhh...

The alarm on her phone buzzed, reminding her she had a meeting to attend. Quickly she typed: *Have to run to a meeting.*

Have fun.

Chapter Nine

On her way home, Delaney stopped at the store and bought groceries, trying to not look at her phone to see if another message had come in without her hearing it.

She dropped the bags on the kitchen table and strode over to the French doors, opening them to the deck. She walked to the far edge and leaned over the railing to shout through her neighbor's open doors. "Luther, you there? Dinner in an hour?"

She couldn't see him but could hear him clearly. "We aren't eating grass again, are we?"

She rolled her eyes. "*One* time I made you a vegetarian dinner, years ago, and you still bitch about it. No, we're having steaks. Good steaks."

"Perfect, see you in an hour. You want beer or wine?"

"Beer. Come on over when you're ready."

Delaney quickly put away the groceries, then made a simple salad, popped two potatoes into the microwave to pre-cook them, and took out the steaks to bring them to room temperature before throwing them on the grill. After switching on some music, she poured herself a very small glass of white wine while she made dressing, knowing that she'd have a beer with dinner, popped bread in the toaster oven, and then set the table. For years—ever since she'd moved in next door to him—she'd had dinner every Wednesday with Luth4er and his wife, Sheila. After Sheila's death to cancer, Luther and Delaney had continued to eat dinner together at least once a week. The older man was the closest thing she had to family in Rhode Island, and she looked forward to their evenings together.

The timer buzzed, letting her know it was time to wrap the potatoes in foil and pop them into the oven to finish cooking. It was a comfort meal, through and through: steak, baked potatoes, salad, and warm sourdough bread. And it was a meal guaranteed to make Luther happy, especially when she pulled out the lemon cupcakes after.

Luther came through the deck door, carrying both a six pack of Corona, and a bottle of Cabernet Sauvignon. "Heya, Lulu."

Delaney grimaced. Luther had called her Lulu since right after their first meeting, saying she reminded him of a childhood friend. "Hi, Luther."

"How was your day?"

They made small talk while Delaney started moving things to the table. "Luther, I'm going out to do the steaks. You okay in here?"

"Of course!"

Out on the deck, Delaney put the meat on the grill, making sure the flames were adjusted properly. Rather than going back inside, she admired her garden as she waited.

Minutes later, she took the steaks off the fire and put them onto the serving platter. She covered them with foil before heading back toward the kitchen. As soon as she opened the door, she could hear Luther's voice. Who was he talking to?

Delaney realized Luther had her cell phone in front of him and was clearly speaking to someone via the speaker. Just then, she heard James' voice come through the phone. Horror filled her! She shouted, "Luther, give me the phone, now."

He shook his head, leaning over the phone on the counter. "Now, Lulu. We're having a great conversation. I just explained that we have dinner together every Wednesday night, and I invited James to join us next week. I told him to bring wine."

Dropping the platter on the counter, Delaney grabbed the phone and turned off the speaker. "Be right with you," she said before covering the microphone, and hissing at Luther, "I will get you!"

He laughed, taking his beer and moving into the living room.

Delaney took a deep breath, then uncovered the phone. "Hi."

She could hear the repressed laughter in James' voice. "Hi. I didn't mean to cause a problem."

"You didn't! Luther knows better than to answer my phone, but he still does it." She tried to calm down. "Sorry. I don't mean to sound grouchy."

"You don't." He paused. "I was just calling to say hi, nothing more."

Warmth spread through her. "I'm glad."

"Then if you're glad, why don't I let you go eat dinner with Luther, then give me a call later if you get bored."

"I'll do that." Delaney looked over her shoulder toward where Luther had gone. "And yes, you're invited to dinner next Wednesday if you want to join us."

Her invitation thrilled James, realizing that it meant she was thinking beyond just drinks too. "That would be great. Luther told me I can bring the wine."

"You can."

Chapter Ten

Sitting down at the table, Delaney waited for Luther to pounce. It only took about five seconds after his first bite. "Perfect steak, Lulu."

"Thanks."

"So? Who is he?" As he asked, his tone was relaxed, but his gaze was laser-fixed on her.

She sighed. She might as well tell him the truth, because she knew damn well he wouldn't rest until he knew it all. "He's a guy I met last Friday. Remember when I told you that I was going to an art show with Pam?"

"Yes. Some modern art thing. You were grumbling about going."

She laughed. "Yeah, I was. Anyway, we went because Pam was interested in him. Pam and I got separated. Then I wandered off. He came up to me, we got talking, but I didn't realize who he was."

"And? How did you go from then to him coming to dinner next Wednesday?"

"He's coming to dinner because you invited him!"

"Because he called you!" He took a sip of his beer. "Continue."

"Anyway, I left the event, but over the weekend he called my office and asked me out. I didn't get the message until

Monday. Then we texted, and I agreed to go to coffee this morning."

"How'd it go?"

She looked down at her plate, aware that she was blushing, "It was great."

"And?"

"Then he asked me out again."

"And you said yes?"

"And I said yes to going for drinks later this week, and we texted each other this afternoon."

"And he called you tonight."

"Yes, and then *you* invited him to dinner."

"I did."

Delaney pushed salad around her plate. "Luther, remember when I was flying back from Chicago last year, and I called you to say I'd given up my seat, and I came back the next morning?"

This seemed to be a non-sequitur. "Yes."

"That was him. He doesn't know it, but it was him."

"What are you talking about?"

"I heard him begging the airline to let him on the flight, something about a family emergency. They couldn't help him, so I gave up my seat. I recognized him immediately the other night, but he doesn't seem to remember it was me that day."

Luther noted, with interest, that Delaney was still blushing as she said this. "So, Lulu. Did you know that you found him attractive before or after you gave up your seat?"

Why deny it? "Probably both. I didn't really get a good look at him until it was done."

"Are you going to tell him?"

She shrugged. "Maybe. If this goes somewhere, then maybe."

After the relaxing dinner with Luther, Delaney slowly cleaned up her kitchen, enjoying the simplicity of the tasks. It was funny, she could feel herself getting excited about the prospect of calling James. When was the last time she'd felt that way? Once the kitchen gleamed she was ready to finally give him a call, but her phone rang and—from the ring tone— she knew it was Pam.

"Hi, Pam."

"Laney! How are you?"

Several minutes of small talk later, Pam said, "So I went out with Thomas."

"And?"

"And he is amazing. Tall, dark, just as handsome as his brother, but so sweet and sexy."

"I'm glad." As she said it, Delaney realized it was true. She was happy for Pam, and even happier that Pam and James hadn't hooked up.

Pam continued, "So it all worked out. I'm glad I connected with Thomas instead of James."

Should Delaney tell her? Was it too early? If her friend found out some other way, there would be hell to pay. "Pam, I need to tell you something."

"Of course! What's up?"

The words came out in a rush. "James asked me out."

"What?" The shock was clear from her voice. "He did what?"

Delaney swallowed and quickly said, "We're going out for drinks this weekend."

"He asked you out?"

Delaney tried hard not to react to the scathing tone in her friend's voice. Clearly, it wasn't sitting well with Pam. It wasn't that James didn't want to go out, it was that he wasn't interested in *her*. Delaney tried to sound nonchalant instead of defensive. "He did. We actually had coffee this morning, and I'm going out with him again this weekend."

"Oh." Pam paused. "That's wonderful, Laney."

"Thank you." Delaney's voice was timid. "Are you okay with this?"

"Of course, I am!" Her voice softened, and Laney could hear the normal warmth. "I mean it. That's wonderful."

After a few more minutes of chitchat, Delaney hung up and sat in silence on the couch. How had she gone from thinking that she was just going out for coffee—nothing more—to having another date with him, messaging him all day, and now having dinner plans with him and Luther for next week?

She flopped back on the couch, putting her legs up on one of the arms, and stared at the ceiling. It had been years since she'd gone out with a man more than twice. After her disastrous marriage, she'd kept dating to a couple first dates a year, maybe one or two second dates. Frankly, she hadn't gone farther than that more than once since her divorce, and that relationship had lasted only a couple weeks. James seemed interested, *really* interested. Was this what she wanted?

She pondered. Was it? Shit, yes. Ever since she'd seen him last year, he'd popped up in her mind once in a while. She'd let herself have the momentary hormonal rush of how he'd looked as he'd walked away from that kiosk. It had been so safe. She could sit and daydream about him, knowing that she would never actually meet him, and now, not only had they met, but he'd asked her out. *Should* she tell him about Chicago? No. That was her own little secret, something she could hold onto as her very own.

She snagged her phone off the coffee table. She had said she would call him, so she should. She dialed and laid back on the couch.

He answered on the second ring, his voice deep. "Hi."

Delaney liked that he clearly knew who was calling. "Hi."

"How was your dinner?"

She laughed. "It was really good, other than Luther pumping me for information."

"Why was he doing that?"

Delaney was glad he couldn't see her face go red suddenly. "Because I don't often have strange men calling me. It was the most exciting thing that's happened to him in months."

"You really don't date?" His voice showed his disbelief.

She snorted. "I went out with you this morning, didn't I?"

"You did."

"But no, I don't. That's what I was telling you. I am so work-focused that my social life is awful, and even when I do take a break, I usually steer clear of dating."

"Why?"

"Because it keeps life simpler."

"Okay. But you said yes to me."

"I did." She laughed. "Don't let it go to your head." She started to cough violently.

James was concerned. "You okay?"

"Yeah." She cleared her throat, and suddenly, her voice was normal again. "I was going to make a smart-ass comment, but tried to keep it in, which made me cough."

The description amused him. "Now I'm intrigued. What was the comment?"

On the couch, Delaney wiggled, suddenly embarrassed. "Pam just called, and my comment was that, while I told you not to let it go to your head, it was going to *mine*."

"Huh?"

"Oh shit, this is probably too much information, but Pam was less than pleased that you weren't interested in *her*. In all our years of friendship, no one has ever chosen me over her, so I have to admit my ego was raging."

His voice deepened, and Delaney immediately felt her body react with a rush of warmth. "Delaney, to be clear, I had no intention of asking *anyone* out at that event. It was something I had to go to, nothing more. But when I met you, I wanted to get to know you, to spend time with you. And if that pisses Pam off, oh well."

"Really?"

"Really." He sighed. "Damn, Delaney, it's *you* I want to spend time with, not her. That's why I called tonight, first because I just wanted to hear your voice, but also to try to convince you to go for drinks before Sunday. I don't care where we go, I don't care what we do, I just want to see you sooner than Sunday."

Warmth filled her, and Delaney realized she was grinning from ear to ear. "Oh."

"*Oh?* That's it? I'm making a begging ass of myself, and all you can say is *oh*?" He suddenly sounded both irritated and unsure of himself.

"No, not just 'oh.'" Delaney swallowed. "'Oh' like I didn't know what to say." She giggled. "I was sitting here grinning like an idiot, and my words deserted me."

"Oh! That kind of 'oh.' I like that kind." Now he sounded pleased. "So, how about it?"

"What?" Delaney had forgotten the question, daydreaming about spending time with him again.

His voice was patient. "Will you go out with me before Sunday?"

For a millisecond, Delaney resisted, not wanting to jump into getting together so soon. She was hoping to keep some boundaries, but the idea of seeing him again was too appealing. "Yes."

In his living room, James pumped his fist, glad no one else could see him. "What works for you?"

The next night was out, but Friday was free. "Friday evening? We could get drinks."

"Great. Where?"

She shrugged, then realized he couldn't see her. "What works for you?" Her brow furrowed. "I don't know where you live."

"Kingston." He thought about the local area. "How about The Seashell? Do you know where it is?"

Delaney laughed. "Yeah, I know where it is. That's perfect."

"What time works for you?"

Delaney thought ahead to the upcoming couple of days, figuring out how early she could leave the office, arrive home, get changed, and make the drive over. "Six?"

"Perfect. I'll call and get us a table on the deck."

"Sounds good."

They talked for a few more minutes, then Delaney stretched. "I need to go get ready for tomorrow." She bit her lip. "Thanks for calling earlier."

"Thanks for calling me back." In his living room, James stood by the glass doors, watching the waves roll in below. "Is it okay if I call you tomorrow?"

She wiggled in happiness. "Absolutely. Anytime between four and six-thirty tomorrow evening works."

"I'll call you then.

Tomorrow and Yesterday

Chapter Eleven

The next day, James sat across the picnic table from his mother, each of them with a cold beer and a lobster roll, a shared order of french fries between them. After a sip and a bite, Gail looked at her son. "Go ahead. You've done your civic duty asking your mother out to lunch. Ask me what you want."

Thank God for intuitive mothers! James shook his head in amazement. "Okay, what do you know about her? I mean really know."

"Assuming we're talking about Delaney?"

"Of course we are!"

She took another sip. "Here's what I know, some from her directly, some from what I have pieced together."

He interjected, "How long have you known her?"

She thought back. "At least eight years."

"Okay. Sorry for interrupting."

"You didn't. You're just impatient, something I rarely see in you." She reached out to squeeze his hand. "I know that she was orphaned quite young. My understanding, although she has never said it directly, is that she lost both her parents at the same time. I don't know if she has siblings. I know she's from somewhere in the Midwest, but she doesn't talk about any of that at all. I mean *at all*. It's like it's sealed off. She went to Brown for undergrad, with a degree in psychology. Then she went to BU for a degree in clinical social work/counseling and got licensed as a special educator. She's lived in Pawtucket since she started at Brown. My understanding is that she moved into a condo when she started college, and that is where she still lives now. She was married—for a very short time—and had a seemingly civil divorce."

"How do you know that?" *She'd been married?* This shocked him, knowing how hesitant she was about dating. Maybe this explained her being cautious.

"She was married to that asshole, Tom Duncan. I've seen them both at social events, and they're able to speak to each other without punches or wine being thrown. Not warm and friendly, but not screaming at each other."

"Tom Duncan? Seriously?" James took a minute to absorb that information. Delaney had been married to a lawyer who was known for both his philandering and his ruthless behavior in court? Wow. The woman who glowed talking about her school had been married to that snake? James tried to re-focus. "Continue."

"She lives alone, works obsessively, and covers overnight crisis on Thursday nights."

"What?" His voice rose in disbelief.

Gail shrugged. "She works the overnight crisis shift at Mercy Hospital on Thursday nights."

He didn't realize his voice was curt. "Why would she do that?"

"She hasn't told me about this, I only know it because Denise works that shift, and knows Delaney pretty well. Denise says she says she does it to keep her clinical license valid, but that she clearly loves the work."

That information rocked James. Little Delaney was working overnight in the busiest emergency room in the area, doing the mental health crisis assessments? If his sister-in-law Denise had said she did, she must, but what a shock to think about it. That explained her time constraints about him calling her tonight, but he still was shocked. She went from working with little kids to suicidal adults high on every possible drug? She was more and more interesting!

Gail's voice was interested. "You look surprised."

"I am." He thought about his reaction. "The first time I met her, she was in a little evening dress and high heels, sipping champagne, looking at art. Frankly, I didn't see her as a public servant. Then we had breakfast yesterday at Sift, and again, she looked every bit the well-educated, financially secure, urban woman, not someone doing safety assessments in a locked ward." His brow furrowed. "As I told you, I tried to cyber-stalk her as much as I could."

"Which isn't much."

"No, it isn't. Other than what's on the school's website, there's very little about her out there. I couldn't find an online footprint at all. No Facebook, no Twitter, nothing. Then we went for coffee yesterday, and she was quick to make sure that she met me there. I didn't pick her up and she insisted on paying for our breakfast. It was pretty clear that she needed to keep boundaries in place."

"So, you did ask her out!"

"Yeah." James quickly filled his mother in. "Then we actually talked on the phone last night, and she agreed to move drinks up to Friday. But getting personal information from her is like pulling teeth."

"I know it is." She dipped a fry in ketchup. "It's not like she's hiding something, it's more like she's closed off her past and doesn't look back."

"Exactly."

She looked at her son. "You like her."

He nodded. "A lot."

Of all her sons, James was the one least likely to talk about his feelings about a woman, so Gail tried to hide her surprise at his strong response. "Talk to me."

He understood what she was asking of him. "Beyond the physical attraction, I like her sense of humor. I like that she clearly has reservations about going out with me but was willing to figure out a way to make it work." He shrugged. "When I called her yesterday, she was making dinner for her neighbor, who clearly is a retired man. They eat together every Wednesday. I like that."

"That's pretty cute."

"And last night she told me that her friend Pam had been tough on her about my asking her out, and it was adorable to hear her voice. She was clearly proud that I asked her out instead of Pam but was embarrassed about it."

"Interesting."

After lunch, James drove his mother home, stopping in the driveway in front of the house. She turned to look at him. "Coming in?"

"No. I'm going to work for a bit and see if I can call Delaney before she goes to work tonight."

Chapter Twelve

On Friday, Delaney drove the familiar route to the Seashell, realizing that she had never been this excited about going there before. Out of habit, she pulled into the back corner of the parking lot—smiling as she recognized many of the staff cars. People worked here for decades; it was almost like a second family for them all. She was excited to see them, and no matter how much she wanted to act like it wasn't impacting her, she couldn't wait to see James again. Taking a final look in the rear visor mirror, she headed to the front instead of the delivery door as she always had. She could see James waiting for her on the front deck, a warm smile on his face. She allowed herself a moment to admire how good he looked in the blazer and button-down shirt.

Standing in front of him, she realized again how he towered over her, even though she was wearing medium heels that evening. "Hi."

He grinned openly. "Hi."

Stepping into the busy restaurant, James put a protective hand on her back, and Delaney had to admit that she liked him touching her. Not moving away, she looked at the hostess, smiling as she recognized her.

"Delaney!" Meg shouted in glee, completely ignoring the customers standing between her and her old friend. "Be right with you, love, give me just a minute." In a completely efficient manner, she grabbed two menus, and guided the older couple ahead of them into the restaurant.

James looked at her quizzically. "Something I should know?"

Delaney shrugged. "I worked here for years when I was in college and grad school."

"Really?"

"Yeah." She grinned at him. "You made a great choice. I love it here."

In less than a minute, the hostess returned, and James watched in amusement as the blue haired woman hugged Delaney hard, chattering away.

Once she'd properly greeted her old friend, Delaney stepped back and took her date's hand. "Meg, this is James. I think he made a reservation for the deck."

Looking quickly at the book, Meg nodded. "Here you are, but—" She rubbed something out and scribbled quickly. "I'm moving you to the end table—better view and more private."

James nodded, impressed. "Thank you."

"My pleasure!"

Within minutes, they were seated at a table looking at the Atlantic, slightly secluded from the rest of the patrons. Meg had disappeared after taking their order for a bottle of wine.

James chuckled. "To get this table, I guess I need to come here with you. I've been here dozens of times, and never get this one."

Tipping her head, Laney felt young, hopeful, and a bit flirtatious—all rare for her. She smiled broadly. "After the millions of miles I walked up and down the stairs here with loaded trays, I *deserve* this table."

"Good to know." A waitress arrived, gave Delaney a hug, then poured the wine.

After the wine had been tasted and approved, James leaned back to look at Delaney intently. "So, my mother says you work the overnight at Mercy."

"I do." She sipped her wine, waiting for him to ask the questions which were clearly building up in him.

"Why?" He looked confused for a moment. "You clearly have a more than full time job."

She shrugged, used to the questions. "Because I love it. I became a social worker because I like to help people figure out how to improve bad situations. I love my day job, but this feeds another part of my soul."

"Really?"

Before he could ask more, an older man came bustling over. James recognized him from the photos in the lobby. He was shocked as the man said something to Delaney in what sounded like Greek. He watched in amazement as she pushed back her chair to give the man a tight hug, chattering back to him in the same language. Still holding his hand, she turned back to the table. "James, this is Nico, owner of the Seashell. Nico, James."

James stood and shook the man's hand. "Nice to meet you. You have an amazing restaurant."

Nico beamed. "And you make beautiful art, James. My wife and I visited your exhibit last week." Then he grinned at Laney. "And you have a beautiful date. Not once before has our Laney ever come here with a man."

James tried to hide his delight. "Thank you." His eyes moved to Delaney. "And yes, I do have a beautiful date."

"Sit, sit, both of you!" Once they were seated again, he tapped Delaney's shoulder. "And the two of you haven't ordered dinner yet, so I'm going to."

Delaney immediately said something sharply to him in Greek. And to James' great amusement, the older man pinched her cheek and said to him, "Laney says the plan was just drinks, but I don't think you'd mind dinner too, would you?"

James tried not to laugh as he saw the look Delaney was giving Nico. "Well, I'd love to have dinner, but I did say it was up to Delaney."

Delaney started to blush, seeing how he was giving her an out. Did she want the evening to end so soon? No, she didn't. "Dinner would be great, thank you."

"I told you so!" Nico beamed.

Delaney gave a retort that made him laugh, and Nico nudged her arm. "Don't make me wash your mouth out with soap, little one." He rubbed his hands together. "I will put in the order."

After he left, James poured more wine into both of their glasses. "Laney, if you want to leave, I understand."

"Do you want to leave?"

"Hell no!"

"Okay! Then let's have dinner!"

Over the next hour and a half, four amazing courses arrived, and the two of them ate, laughed, and talked. James learned about how she had worked there all through college and grad school, learning Greek along the way. As the evening wore on, he was thrilled to see how she relaxed, and he could see more of the spirit and sense of humor his mother had talked about.

The night was growing dark as they finished their coffee and baklava. When the waitress came back for their dishes, James asked her for the check. She handed him the familiar black portfolio, opening it as he pulled out his wallet. He raised one eyebrow as he looked at Delaney. "You're a cheap date, lady."

She was confused. "What do you mean?"

With a chuckle, he handed her the check, and she saw Nico's familiar scrawl on the bill: *Dinner was my idea, and my little Laney looks happier than I've ever seen her. All the best, Nico.*

The bill was for just the bottle of wine they had ordered when they arrived.

Delaney shook her head. "The meddling pain in the ass." She reached out and touched his hand. "Are you okay with this?"

"Of course I am." He grinned wickedly. "Just means that so far, I still haven't bought you dinner, so now you need to go out with me again."

"Deal."

Tomorrow and Yesterday

Chapter Thirteen

After goodbyes with the staff, they walked out to the parking lot, and James was surprised when she took his hand without saying a word. At her car, she leaned back and looked up at him, still holding his hand. "I had a really good time, thank you."

"Me too."

Before he could say that he wanted to see her the next day, she said in a rush, "Would you like to do something tomorrow?"

Leaning down, he stroked the side of her face. "I'd love to."

She grinned with relief, and he realized that she'd been nervous asking. "What do you want to do?"

"Anything."

She squeezed his hand. "How about the Cliff Walk? I was going to go last weekend, but never got around to it."

"Perfect." He thought about the logistics. "Want to meet at Sift tomorrow morning for breakfast, then go to the Cliff Walk from there?"

"I'd like that."

"What time?"

"I'm up early." Immediately, he could see her start to blush and she looked down at her feet. "I mean, whatever works for you."

He moved closer. "Laney, look at me." She did, slowly. "I'll meet you as early as you want and stay as late as you want. Okay?"

"Okay." She rose on her tiptoes and kissed his cheek. "Thanks for a great evening, and I'll see you tomorrow at 8?"

"See you then."

Chapter Fourteen

By noon the next day, Delaney knew she was in over her head. Every moment she was with James, she found herself feeling more and more for him, like a teenager with a crush. This was so unlike her, and she needed to find her footing again!

As they finished their walk and were talking about going for a late lunch, they heard a female voice call out. "Mr. McDaniels? You are James McDaniels, aren't you?"

The voice belonged to a gorgeous young woman who had run by them just a minute earlier. Delaney had noticed her in the way that women automatically compare each other. The runner's body was showcased in leggings and a cropped top, her long blonde hair pulled back in a messy ponytail. All in all, she was spectacular, Delaney realized in dismay.

The woman ran up to James, smiling at him seductively, clearly used to men noticing her.

While the stranger gushed at James about his art, and made sure her interest in him was clear, Delaney moved to the side of the trail, looking out over the Atlantic. Trying to keep her emotions in check, she started counting waves to keep her mind calm. It was too soon for her to be reacting like this! Jealousy was a useless emotion, one that she need not allow herself. Yeah, right.

She was so intent on the waves, and trying to control her inner turmoil, she didn't hear James come up behind her. She jumped when she felt his strong fingers start to gently massage the base of her neck. She didn't turn, or say a word, just kept trying to focus on the waves.

His voice was gentle and quiet, just loud enough that only she could hear him. "So, what just happened?"

She still didn't turn but tipped her head slightly so his talented fingers could keep working on her tight neck muscles. Her voice was guarded. "What do you mean?"

"I mean, one minute you were standing near me, then you were gone—like you weren't with me at all."

Her voice became defensive. "I just moved to the side so you could talk to that woman."

His tone didn't change. "Bullshit. You walked away and didn't look back." He paused. "Like you did the night we met. Is that what you want? To walk away and not look back?"

It took everything in her not to pull away from him, but for a split second she realized that this mattered, and that she needed to tell him the truth. "No. I didn't know what to do. I felt completely out of place, I…"

"You…?"

Her voice was rushed. "I didn't know what to do! This is too new. I didn't know what you wanted me to do, and I just felt like the best thing was to get the hell out of the way."

He leaned down and placed a soft kiss where his fingers had been mere seconds before. "What I wanted you to do? I wanted you to stay close enough to me that I could have my arm around you or hold your hand." She could hear the humor in his voice. "I wanted you to stay and stake your claim."

"Really?"

"Really." His fingers went back to massaging the base of her neck, and he smiled as he felt her lean back a bit, almost resting against him. "I know this is new, Laney, I get it. But all I want is for you to give it a chance."

"I'm trying to!"

"I know you are. But if you sense another woman is coming into what you see as your territory, don't run. Stand your ground." He nuzzled her ear. "If I thought someone was coming on to you, you can bet I wouldn't walk away."

With that, she leaned back against him. "I'm not good at this."

"What? Cuddling with me? You're doing just great." As he said this, his arms came around her, and she realized how very much she liked being there.

She elbowed him in the abdomen, not surprised when she met solid muscle. "No, wise ass. This is so new; I feel like an idiot."

"Then we figure it out as we go."

She paused. "Okay."

He pulled her in closer to his body. "Since we're almost done with our walk, what do you want to do?"

She looked out at the waves, her heart racing and her voice tentative. "I want to spend the rest of the day with you."

She couldn't see the grin that immediately spread across his face. "That was the answer I was hoping for." He barely rested his chin on the top of her head, enjoying how they fit together. "So here are some options. We can go into Newport and get something to eat, we can go back to Providence and do the same, or we can go to my place and I will make you a late lunch-early dinner."

Feeling bold, Delaney turned around and stretched up to put her arms around his neck. "How about we go to your place and make dinner together?"

James tried to ignore how quickly his body responded as her breasts pressed against his chest. "Sounds like a plan."

When they got back to the parking lot, James looked at their two cars in dismay. "Do you want to follow me, or I can bring you back here later to get your car?"

"I'll follow you."

Chapter Fifteen

As she drove behind him, Delaney tried to not let her hopes get too high. Yes, he was beautiful, smart, funny, sexy, and seemed kind and sensitive. But really, what did she know about him? Her ex-husband had seemed like a real catch too! Just then his blinker went on, and he was pulling into a gated driveway.

The house before her was spectacular; not too big, not too small. It was perched on a small hill overlooking the ocean, stone retaining walls overflowing with bright flowers. It was gorgeous.

Pulling into the parking space across from the garage, Delaney got out of the car slowly. Okay, it was time to take a step back. For a few short seconds as she had pulled in, she had thought of how she could see herself living here. Too soon to be thinking like that! They had only met eight days before, and this was really only their third date. It was way too soon to be thinking about anything more than this evening.

Yeah, right...

James was waiting for her by the walkway, wondering about that grave expression she was wearing. What was she thinking about? As he speculated, he let his eyes roam over her, seeing the blush on her cheekbones from the sun and wind. He also noticed her hair was more wildly curly than normal and that her capris and t-shirt fit her beautifully. He had to admit, her casual wear was even sexier than the dress she'd been wearing when they first met.

When she walked over to him, he saw the serious look leave her eyes as she said, "Why, hello there."

"Hello there."

"You know, you broke several speeding laws on your way here."

"Really?" He took her hand, leading her toward the side door of the house.

"Really."

He looked at her with a gleam in his eyes. "Maybe that was because I couldn't wait to get you here."

That answer made her heart race even more. "Well, then I guess it was justified."

Stepping into the house, Delaney felt like she'd come home. It was exactly what she would design for herself. Huge windows facing the ocean, soft, neutral colors, comfortable furniture. Looking around, she felt herself relax. "James, it's beautiful."

"Thank you." He put his arm around her. "I'm glad you like it."

"I really do."

"Then come see the rest." Taking her hand, he walked her room by room through the house, stopping to let her explore. Standing in the door of his bedroom, Delaney looked out at the two walls of windows, and let herself visualize what it would be like to wake up next to him in that room. His voice was sexy. "You can go in, you know. I promise to behave, but you're welcome to look around."

Not letting go of his hand, she stepped into the room, noticing a wingback chair tucked in the corner by the window.

It was positioned outward, placed just so the occupant would have the best view of the ocean. "That's the perfect place for a chair."

"I know, isn't it?" He touched her face. "Any time you want, that chair is yours."

"Thank you."

"Want to see my office and studio?"

"Yes, please."

Walking to the other end of the house, James opened a door, and gestured inside. "My office."

It was a purely masculine space with its huge wooden desk, shelves loaded with legal tomes, rich dark colors, and leather chairs. Delaney ran her hand over the edge of one of the chairs, feeling the buttery soft leather. "How often do you practice law?"

He shrugged. "Probably like your work at Mercy. It's not my primary focus anymore, but I still love it, and I take on pro bono cases that I believe in."

"Oh." The man was more and more interesting. "And your studio?"

"This way." Stepping out of his office, James led the way down a short hallway, past a half-bath, and then opened a sliding barn door.

The space was huge. Light streamed in from the three walls of glass and the skylights. Easels were arranged around the room, holding works in varying stages of completion. A massive center table had a neatly organized array of brushes, sketch pads, and paints.

Without saying a word, Delaney started walking around the room. James leaned on the table, watching her. She stopped at each canvas, alternating between studying them intently and looking beyond to the breathtaking view of the ocean and the flowers outside. "They're beautiful."

He chuckled. "You mean for modern art."

She shook her head, still moving, headed toward his most recent work. "No, they're beautiful. Just because it's not my favorite style doesn't mean that I can't appreciate them." She stopped, entranced by the final work. "Wow."

"Do you like it?"

"I do. I..." Delaney was speechless, caught by the raw emotion of the painting. She was struck by the beauty of the lines and swirling colors, sensing such a power of caring in it. "It's amazing."

He came to stand behind her, wrapping his arms around her like he had on their walk. "I'm glad you like it." He kissed her temple. "You're the inspiration."

"What?" Her first emotion was shock, but it was quickly replaced by a rush of pride.

"Yes, this was all you. The night after we met, I came home and painted for hours." He reached out to trace the long sensual line that ran down the canvas. "That was you in your little dress last Friday." He touched the eddy of tints that had grabbed her attention. "Those were the colors you were wearing at breakfast." He gestured to the outer corner of the canvas. "That's how I felt when you said yes to going out with me."

Delaney turned around so she could look at him, her eyes glowing. "That's amazing. I absolutely love it." She reached up, pulling his head down. "I've never been the inspiration for a painting before, thank you." She kissed him.

The touch of her lips rocked James more than he would have expected. Since the first moment he saw her, he'd known that he wanted her, but kissing her was so much more than he'd thought it would be.

He pulled her close, wrapping his arms around her as she tightened her hold on him, desire racing through both.

The kiss lasted for long moments, where both lost track of time. It was the clanging of the grandfather clock that interrupted them. Reluctantly, he loosened his arms, "Wow."

She smiled, slightly dazed. "Wow, indeed."

Tomorrow and Yesterday

Chapter Sixteen

In the kitchen, James motioned to a stool. "Take a seat and keep me company."

"I can help."

He grinned as he reached up to take down two wine glasses, then paused. "Wine or beer?"

"Wine, please."

He continued, "Here's the deal. If you sit there, I may get dinner cooked. You help me, and I'm going to be spending every minute trying to get you back in my arms and dinner will be ruined."

She laughed. "I highly doubt it."

With lightning speed, he put the glasses down and came around the counter, pressing her back against the cool marble, an arm on either side of her. His kiss was sure, and again, deepened almost instantly. When he pulled back, he grinned down at her. "Did I make my point?"

"You did." She pulled out a stool and sat down. "But even if you're cooking, you can still do that…"

He kissed her forehead. "My pleasure." Snagging a corkscrew, he pulled a bottle of chilled white from the wine fridge, opened it, and poured some for each of them. Raising his glass, he looked at her. "Thank you for a perfect day."

"Thank *you*!"

While he pulled ingredients out and started cooking, the conversation stayed light. Following his directions to find utensils and napkins, Delaney set the table for them, then wandered back behind the island to where he was stirring the sauce for the pasta. He looked sideways at her, seeing the mischievous look on her face. "Getting brave, aren't you?"

She tried to look innocent. "I'm just checking on dinner."

"How's it look?"

"Good."

She was so busy trying to pay attention to the stove, she missed when he put the spoon down and moved to quickly pick her up and set her on the counter. Eye to eye, he looked at her. "Yeah, it does look good." He leaned forward, his lips stopping just before he kissed her. "You look amazing." He nuzzled her neck. "You smell amazing." He kissed her. "You taste amazing."

She tried to hold back a happy giggle. He noticed, and raised one eyebrow, which made her laugh outright. "What's so funny?"

"It's not funny." She reached out to grasp the front of his shirt, pulling him closer. "I'm happy."

"Me too." Stroking her face, he rubbed the pad of his thumb across her lower lip, his eyes darkening with desire as he saw her body respond to his touch. His voice was soft. "Laney?"

"Yes?"

He took a deep breath, and a half step back, needing to put some space between them. "You'll tell me if I'm moving too fast, right?"

She was touched. "I will."

"I mean, shit, I get it. We met just over a week ago, and I know that I've been relentless."

Grinning, she reached out to pull him closer again. "James, I really appreciate that. And yes, I get that I was the one who made us wait, but I was the one who asked you to do something today." She leaned forward so she could rest her forehead against his. "And as I remember it, I was the one who really kissed you first."

He moved so that he could lightly tickle her sides, making her wiggle. "Yes, you were. So really, I'm the injured party here. You're the one rushing me."

She licked her lips, seeing how his eyes immediately moved to them. "Injured party? Well, if I'm rushing you…" She moved to jump off the counter, thrilled when he held her in place. "I'll slow down."

"You stay right there." He turned and grabbed her glass of wine, handing it to her. "I was wrong. Having you over there was distracting me. Having you right here is better."

When the dishes were done and put away, they walked down the hill toward the ocean to sit and watch the sunset. Delaney knew she needed to start home, or she was going to give in to temptation and stay for the night. No matter how much she liked James, no matter how physically attracted she was to him, it was too soon to take that step.

She didn't realize that she'd let out such a long breath until James asked, "What's the sigh for?" His voice was gentle, and he squeezed her hand.

Delaney felt the immediate jump of her heart. "I need to head home soon."

"You can stay, you know that, right?"

"I guess I assumed that, but…"

"But it's too soon. I get it, I just wanted you to know the invitation stands."

She stood and tugged his hand, so he was standing as well. "Thank you." She wrapped her arms around him and leaned against his chest. "Know that I want to. Know that it's taking every ounce of my will power to say I need to go home."

James rubbed her back, loving the feeling of her in his arms. "Understood." He kissed her hair. "How about you let me drive you home? I hate the idea of you making the drive alone."

She laughed. "I can drive home alone." She grinned. "Besides, if I'm going to be coming here once in a while, I should get to know the route."

"Once in a while? How about tomorrow?"

Taking his hand again, Delaney started walking back to the house. "Hey, mister, I still need to do my job, you know. I never take a whole Saturday off. I need to do some work tomorrow." Before he could respond, she turned to look at him. On the hill, she stood slightly higher; they were almost eye to eye. "How about you come see me tomorrow, and let me make you dinner?"

"But you're making me dinner on Wednesday. How about I bring dinner over to make your life easier?"

"That would work."

After collecting her bag and keys from inside the house, they walked to her car in silence. Delaney unlocked her car and opened the door, letting out the trapped heat. Taking both of his hands, she looked up at him. "I had a really good time today. Thank you."

"Me too." He smiled as she reached her arms up and encircled his neck. "I wish you weren't leaving."

"Me too." She kissed him briefly. "But I'll see you tomorrow. I'll text you the directions so you can GPS my house."

"And you'll call or text me when you get home, so I know you're there safely." It was an order, not a request, but it still made Delaney's heart flutter happily.

"I will."

He leaned down, pulling her close, and kissed her. When he felt her fingers weaving through his hair, he tried to control his rising desire. He pulled back, shook his head, and growled, "Laney, get in the car and drive away, or I may just throw you over my shoulder and keep you here for the night."

She got into the driver's seat and looked up at him. "I'll stay, soon. Just not yet."

James leaned into the car and kissed her quickly. "I know. Drive safe and I'll see you tomorrow."

After a quick shower, Delaney climbed into bed; tired and happy. When was the last time she'd had such a perfect twenty-four hours? She actually couldn't remember when she'd had such a wonderful time.

As she drifted off, she couldn't have been more content, which was why it was so startling when she awoke to the frightened racing of her heart and the cold sweat dampening her skin. In her dreams, she'd seen Jakie running into the cornfield, tears running down his face as he called her name...

Chapter Seventeen

By Tuesday night, Delaney realized that she was completely infatuated with James. She found herself looking at her cell phone almost constantly to see if he'd messaged her. She'd felt like a teenager waiting for him to call the night before, and she had planned and re-planned the menu for Wednesday's dinner a dozen times.

Needing to take a break from her own obsessiveness, she left her phone on the coffee table and walked out onto her back deck, climbing into the hammock.

She heard Luther's voice and realized he'd been sitting on his deck the whole time. "Hey, Lulu. What's on your mind?"

"Why do you think something's on my mind?"

"You never get in the hammock at this time of day on a weekday unless your brain is racing. What's going on?"

"You know you're a pain in the ass, right?" For a moment, she was irritated by his correct assessment of the situation.

"Of course."

She sighed. "Want to come over so I can see your face?"

Within a minute, he'd settled himself in the chair next to her, his feet up on the little table. "Talk to me."

Delaney looked at the darkening sky. "I really like him, Luther. And I don't know what to do about it."

"James." It wasn't a question; it was a statement. "He clearly likes you, too, so what's the problem?"

Luther was the only person in her life with whom she could be completely open. He knew everything. "I think I like him too much. Luther, shit, I like him, *so* much. I want to be with him all the time. I almost stayed overnight with him last weekend. I don't do things like that. It's not how I was raised, and yet, I'm desperate to be with him. I feel like a friggin' idiot, checking my phone constantly to see if he's sent me a message. I didn't go for a run last night because I wanted to be home for his call. I'm losing my normal boundaries."

"Lulu, my love. Your upbringing? Not saying it was wrong, but let it go. You're a successful, independent woman. You need to lose those old rules."

"But what if he finds it out?"

"Not to toot my own horn, but I was a damn fine detective, and for me—even with my connections—it was hard for me to put it all together. He's not going to be able to do it. The only way he'll know is if you tell him." He rubbed his temple. "Even if he did, it wouldn't change his feelings for you, I know it wouldn't." He paused, searching for words. "Sweetheart, you were married to a man without telling him who you really are. You kept a secret for your entire marriage. This is different. You're so much more emotionally connected to James than you ever were to Tom, even after such a short time. You never acted like an idiot, as you put it, with him, other than marrying him against our recommendations."

Delaney rolled her eyes. "I know, I know. You and Sheila were right, I was wrong to marry Tom"

"Good to hear you say it again." He took a sip of the water he'd brought with him. "You never lost yourself in a good way with him. You always kept yourself slightly apart. If James is making you want that level of connection, that's an incredible thing." His voice wobbled. "There was nothing that Sheila didn't know about me. I wanted her to know me inside and out. If that's what you want with James, that's incredible."

"But I've only known him for less than two weeks!"

"And what did we tell you about when we got engaged?"

"That you proposed on the second date." Delaney smiled, remembering the story. "Your first date was a blind date with another couple. Your second date was going to the movies, just the two of you. That's when you proposed, and she said yes."

"And we had a great marriage."

Delaney smiled, rolling on her side so she could see Luther through the hammock roping. "I've never told anyone about my past."

"You told me."

"No, you figured it out, and kept poking at it until I finally gave in and told you what you already knew."

"Fair enough." He looked at her. "It's nothing to be ashamed of, you know."

"It's not something to be proud of either!"

"I disagree, Lulu. You should be proud, *damn* proud, of the life you've made, of the people you've helped. Yes, you lived through hell, but it didn't break you; it made you the strongest person I know."

"Okay, stop. I don't want to talk about that right now. What I want to talk about is: am I rushing this?"

He chuckled. "No. You aren't, Lulu. If he's your forever love, you should get on it without delay. Life is too short as it is."

The next night, Delaney peered into her bedroom mirror, wondering if she looked too much like a 1950's housewife. Her sundress was partially covered by a cooking apron, although she had to admit that the apron actually showed off her curves pretty darn well. One more quick swipe of mascara, and a check of her lip gloss, and she was ready.

Luther was sitting out on her deck, chatting with her through the open door. The table was set and the paella almost ready when Delaney heard a knock at the door. With a quick twist toward the deck, she hissed, "Luther, behave yourself."

He laughed. "If I like him, you have nothing to worry about."

More nervous than she would have expected, Delaney opened the door to find James standing there, two bottles of wine in one hand, the other hand behind his back. She smiled. "Hi."

"Hi." He leaned down and kissed her quickly, then pulled a gorgeous bouquet of flowers from behind his back. "For you."

Delight filled Delaney. She took the bouquet and gazed up at him with glowing eyes. "Thank you!"

"My pleasure."

She realized they were still standing in the doorway. "Come in!"

She took the bottles of wine from him and put them on the counter in the kitchen, then said, "Let me find a vase."

"Just a minute." He pulled her into his arms and kissed her thoroughly, smiling as he felt her pull him closer. Pulling back, he stroked her cheek. "That's better. Two whole days without kissing you is too damn long."

She traced the button placket on his shirt. "It is."

He could see how flustered she was and decided the chivalrous thing would be to change the subject. "Okay, point me in the direction of a vase."

She shook her head slightly, as if trying to clear it. "The cupboard over the fridge, and you can probably reach it without needing to climb on the counter like I would."

With a wicked grin, he looked at her bare legs. "Laney, don't tempt me. You climbing on the counter in that dress is more than I can take right now."

She swatted his arm. "Get the vase and come meet Luther, then I'll show you around."

As she walked back into the kitchen to get a glass of seltzer, Laney realized how happy she was. Luther and James had hit it off immediately, and over dinner, they had realized they had worked on some of the same cases when Luther was a detective and James was a junior prosecutor. Now, they were in the living room, watching the Red Sox, laughing and chatting.

As she was lost in thought, sipping the bubbly water, she felt familiar fingers start massaging her neck. She leaned back against James, smiling as he wrapped his arms around her and kissed her temple. "Hi. Everything okay?"

"Really okay." She squeezed his arms. "I was just standing here feeling happy."

"Good. I *always* want you to be happy."

Luther stayed for a while after dinner, but when he was ready to go, he stood up and stretched. "Okay, kids. I'm going home to watch the last couple innings." He stuck out his hand to James. "It was great to meet you."

"You too."

After he left, James looked down at Laney, who had gotten up to hug the older man goodbye. "Do you need some sleep?"

She was getting to know what his questions really meant. "No, I want to be with you." She gestured at the TV. "Do you want to watch the rest of the game, or sit on the deck or what?"

He walked over to the couch and sat back down. "What I want is for you to come over here and snuggle with me. We can sort of watch the game while we make out like teenagers."

With a giggle, she walked toward him, and knelt on the couch beside him. "That was a pretty detailed plan."

"Mind like a steel trap…" He reached out and stroked one of the straps of her sundress. "And, now that we're alone, let me tell you how absolutely gorgeous you look tonight."

For a moment, he could see a flash of insecurity, then a blush of pride. "Really?"

"Really." He hooked a finger under the strap to pull her toward him and smiled when her body came in contact with his. "Let me show you."

His kiss was warm and sure. Without realizing what she was doing, Laney moved closer, so that she was sitting on his lap, fully encircled by his arms. Her arms wrapped around his neck; her fingers entwined in his hair. The kiss deepened, and Laney felt his hands lightly stroking her back. She ached for him to touch her bare skin, but her mind screamed that it was still too soon to get that intimate with him!

She pulled back slightly and framed his face in her hands. She gazed into his dark eyes, seeing the heat glowing in them. "You know, you're wreaking havoc with my hormones."

He grinned victoriously. "Am I?" He leaned closer to nip at her lower lip and saw her shiver. "Tell me more."

"I don't think so!" She shook her head at him. "Absolutely not! Just telling you that much makes me blush."

With a low growl, he leaned down to nibble on her neck, fighting the urge to stroke her breasts as he saw her nipples tighten with the touch of his lips. "Then wait until you tell me how much you want us to make love."

Her eyes widened in shock. Then she saw the warmth in his dark eyes and felt a rush of desire. It might be currently premature, but soon she was going to enjoy every minute of getting this beautiful man naked. She leaned forward. "Then *you'll* blush."

"Baby, I never blush…"

Tomorrow and Yesterday

Chapter Eighteen

As they watched the game—stopping often to kiss—Delaney leaned against him, loving the feeling of being surrounded by his body. Had she ever felt this safe and wanted? No.

She wasn't really paying attention to what she was doing as she stretched, trying to loosen a tight muscle in her shoulder that had been bothering her for the last couple days. It was definitely time for a couple yoga classes and probably a massage.

His voice was deep and quiet. "What's the matter?"

"A tight muscle, nothing more." She shrugged, resting her head on his shoulder, playing with his hair. "I'm sure I just slept wrong."

He sat up fully, still keeping her on his lap. "Here, come sit cross-legged next to me."

"What?"

He patted the couch cushion next to him. "Come sit here for a couple minutes. I can help."

She moved, although she was completely confused. "What are you talking about? You're a masseuse too?"

He laughed. "Yes."

She looked over her shoulder at him in complete disbelief. "No, you aren't!"

He kissed her bare shoulder. "Delaney, there are still a lot of things we don't know about each other. One thing you don't know about me is that to piss my father off, I trained as a massage therapist."

"What are you talking about?" As she asked, strong fingers started working at her neck and then her shoulders.

He continued, "When I was a senior in college, I told my dad that I didn't want to go into law after all, and that I wanted to go into art."

Really? That got her attention. "And he didn't take it well?"

"He told me that he'd rather have a massage therapist as a son than an artist, so I decided to get him back and got fully trained. I used the money I made to pay for art school while he paid for law school."

"He was at your opening, wasn't he? Does he still not like the art?" As she finished speaking, his fingers moved so that the tight muscle loosened, and she sighed in pleasure.

He kissed her neck. "Laney, you make that sound again, and all bets about being a gentleman are off." He continued to work on the muscle. "That's the funny thing, after I made my point about going to massage school, he got over it, and he's is my biggest fan now."

"That's good." James' phone buzzed with a text, and without changing what he was doing, he looked at the screen and made a derisive sound. Delaney tried to focus on something other than how good his fingers were making her feel. "What's the matter?"

"Speaking of the devil. That's my dad, again."

"Everything okay?"

"Fine. He's just perseverating because he doesn't like when he doesn't get his way." As he spoke, his fingers moved back up to her neck. "Okay, here's my professional opinion, and not just as the man who wants to get you naked. Too much stress, probably too much working on a computer. Either"—he ran light kisses up her neck— "you need to let me work on loosening your muscles on a more regular and longer basis..."

Damn, that sounded good! Delaney tried to concentrate. "Or?"

"Go back to yoga class and commit to not working so much."

"No going for a massage?"

With a laugh, he pulled her back onto his lap suddenly, kissing her hard. Gone were the gentle kisses of earlier. This was a kiss of pure white-hot desire. When he pulled back, he looked at her intently. "Doing the politically correct thing, if you want to go for a massage, go." He kissed her again. "But to be blunt, I'd ask that it be given by a woman." He looked uncomfortable. "My ego can stand you saying you're not ready for me to do it, but another man touching you, even in a professional setting, would push my buttons."

Delaney stroked his lips with her finger, so absorbed in tracing them that she didn't notice how his gaze had intensified. "James, first of all, if I was going to someone other than you for a massage, I wouldn't have a male do it, no matter what." She looked down, and blushed. "James, look, oh shit..." She stood up quickly before he could stop her, moved to stand by the window, and looked out at the now quiet neighborhood.

He came to stand behind her, his hands resting lightly on her shoulders. "Talk to me."

Her arms were wrapped tightly around her abdomen in a protective gesture. "James, here's the thing, and I might as well say it now." She took a deep breath, so deep her entire body trembled with the effort. "I wouldn't have a male masseuse because that wasn't the way I was raised."

His tone was cautious, not wanting to push her away, but shocked that she would talk about her past at all. It had been clear that was a verboten topic. "Okay."

"I went to Brown never having been kissed, or at least not by choice." For a split second, she felt the fear she'd felt when one of her supposed foster brothers had forcibly kissed her. She tried to focus on the conversation. "When I was a freshman in college, I got drunk and had sex for the first time. I only knew his first name, I don't remember it much at all other than it hurt, and that was the end of it. I didn't have sex again until Tom and I were engaged. Then, after I found out he was leaving me, I did the get-drunk-have-sex-with-a-complete-stranger-thing one more time. Then, two years ago, I dated a guy for a little while." She paused. "A really little while, but yes, we did eventually have sex."

"Okay…" He didn't know what to say.

"I want you to know that I get why you wouldn't want to have me go to a guy for a massage, and I wouldn't, but I just needed to explain." On the last anguished word, her hands came up to cover her face.

Gently, he wrapped his arms around her, pulling her into his warmth. He kissed her cheek chastely. "Laney, listen to me carefully."

"I am."

"I want you. I've not hidden that, and I'm not ashamed of it. I also, absolutely, will not force you, and I promise to not push you." At his words, he could feel her relax a tiny bit in his arms. "Laney?"

"Yes."

"Do you want me? Do you want to see where this can go?"

Her answer was quick. "I so do."

"Both?"

"Both."

"Would you please turn around?" She turned and looked up at him shyly. "Laney, I like you. I get that this is fast. I get that we've only known each other for such a short time, and this isn't my normal behavior. In every single—I mean *every* single—relationship I've ever had before, I've been the cautious one, the one who waited to see where it was heading." He paused, realizing something. "In fact, I may have been an ass to women, making them chase me." He looked down at her, his eyes shining. "But not this time. I want to be with you. I want to hear your voice. I want to do great big exciting things with you, and I want to do the little mundane things like just watching the Sox together." He pulled her closer. "And as much as I physically want you, it isn't just a physical thing."

"Oh."

He grinned, although he seemed a bit nervous. "There you go with that *oh* again. What does this one mean?"

"It means that's exactly how I feel too." She leaned her head against his chest. "And I'm so glad you said it, because I couldn't find the words."

He hugged her. "Glad I could help." Kissing her hair, his next words were careful. "Do you ever talk about your distant past?"

Delaney fought the urge to pull back, and instead sighed. "Maybe someday."

"You don't have to, love."

She decided it was time to resort to humor. "So, if I can't go hire some hot guy to give me a massage, does this mean I can ask you to make house calls?"

"Day or night, just call."

Chapter Nineteen

After saying goodnight and making him promise to text her when he got home, Delaney finished tidying up, making sure everything was put together for both school and work at Mercy Hospital for the next day. Then, she changed into her favorite camisole and leggings before climbing into bed and turning on her reading light.

She had read two chapters and was feeling sleepy when her phone buzzed with a text. *Still awake? I'm home.*

She smiled and typed: *Still awake. Call if you want.*

The phone rang seconds later. Her laughter was clear as she answered, "Such patience on your part."

"That's me, Mr. Patience." He cleared his throat. "I know it's late, but I have two ideas." He paused. "Actually, three ideas."

"Okay."

"First, how about I bring over take-out on Friday night, and fix your shoulder. You know, nothing more than a medical house call."

Her tone was dry. "If it's nothing more than a medical house call, forget it."

"How about I rephrase it by saying I can't wait to see you again, and fixing your shoulder is the best excuse I could think of to get you in my arms again soon?"

"Much better, and yes, that sounds great."

"Second, are you doing something on Saturday? I know you said you had work to do that day, but could you move it around?"

"Maybe, why?"

"How about you and I and Luther go to a game in Boston?"

"Hello, tickets?"

"Already taken care of. That is, if you want to go."

"I'd love to."

His voice sounded unsure. "Do you want to ask Luther, or should I?"

For a moment, that question took her breath away, as she understood the underlying sentiment. He knew how important Luther was to her, and he wanted to make sure he did things in a way that would make Luther happy! "He'd love it if you called him. I'll send you his number."

"Perfect. I'll call him tomorrow and let you know what he says."

"He'll say yes but let me know for sure." She wiggled to find a more comfortable spot. "And third?"

"You know how my Dad was texting me tonight?"

"Yeah, you said he was perseverating."

"Well, he's been bugging me about going to the firm's summer event, and I'd been trying to avoid it."

"Why were you avoiding it?"

"Because social events like that make my teeth hurt."

"Okay. And?"

"And as I drove home, I realized that I want to go if you'll go with me." He chuckled. "How about it?"

"When is it?"

"Not this Friday, but next."

"And what's the event?"

He sighed. "It's a semi-formal event at the Newport Country Club—cocktails, dinner, young lawyers sucking up to partners, big clients, etc." He tried to sound nonchalant. "You don't have to go, Laney."

She laughed. "James, I'm happy to go. Just wanted to know when it was, and where, so I knew how to dress."

"You'll go?" He sounded surprised.

"Absolutely." She climbed out of bed and went to her closet. "Now I need to think clothes."

"You'll look gorgeous no matter what you wear." He paused, suddenly realizing something. "Pam may be going too."

"Great. Then I'll know someone there other than you and your mom." She thought for a second. "It sounds like fun. I'd love to go with you."

In her dream, she was riding Freedom through the pasture, wearing a long flowing white dress. When she awoke, her cheeks were wet with tears. Rolling over, she pulled the pillow into her arms, curling around it in a fetal position. She whispered, "Free, I miss you so much."

Tomorrow and Yesterday

Chapter Twenty

Sunday night, Delaney climbed into bed, tired but happy. What a wonderful weekend! The three of them had a blast at the game, and Luther had given his highest praise when he and Delaney were alone for a moment.

"I like this boy," Luther had said. "He understands a pitch count, knows you don't drink fancy beer at the Sox, sings along to Sweet Caroline, and looks at you like you're a princess. He's a keeper."

Thinking back, Delaney smiled as she remembered that on Sunday, she'd felt compelled to work in the morning, and then had been down when she realized how much she missed James. Just as she'd been about to message him—wanting to see if he was around so she could drive over and see him, even if just for a few minutes—he'd called.

"Hi!" She laughed. "I was just about to send you a message."

"You were? What was it going to say?"

"That I wondered if you were home. I was going to drive over because I miss you."

In his car, James chuckled. "Great minds think alike. I was coming back from setting up at the gallery, and I took a detour. I'm parked outside your house."

Joy filled her. "You are?"

"I am." He smiled as she came to the window and waved. "Come get in the car with me and let's picnic on Colt Drive."

"I'll be right there."

Yes, it had been the perfect weekend.

Chapter Twenty-one

The night of the law firm's event, Delaney stood in front of her full-length mirror, looking at her reflection, turning each way to check her appearance from every angle. She shouted, "So, I need to you to be brutal. Anything you think I should change, be honest. I want to make a really good impression on his family."

Luther's voice was wry. "Have I ever been anything but honest?"

"No, you haven't."

"Then get out here."

Delaney walked into the living room, holding her breath. Luther looked her up and down, motioning for her to turn around so he could see her back. Then a slow, wide smile crossed his face. "Lulu, I have never seen you look this good, even on your wedding day. Sweetie, you're spectacular."

"Really?"

Luther stood up, crossed the room, and held out his arms. Delaney hugged him hard, and he held her face in his hands. "Absolutely, Lulu. That outfit is stunning, and you look happy. You are going to wow them."

She took a deep breath and stood up straight. "Thank you."

"You're welcome." He looked at his watch. "He'll be here in a couple minutes. Do you want me to leave before he gets here?"

"No. He loves to see you. Stay."

He patted his pocket. "And will you let an old man take a picture of the two of you before you go out?"

She laughed. "I'd like that."

Five minutes later, they heard a knock on the door. Luther waved his hand. "Go get the door, and that way you get a moment or two alone before I intrude."

Delaney opened the door, and felt her lungs constrict with her first view of James. Standing on her top step, he was dressed in a perfectly tailored summer weight dark-gray suit, pure white shirt, and dark-patterned tie. He was gorgeous, and she realized her voice was breathless as she said, "Hi."

Looking down at her, James felt like he'd been hit by a sledgehammer. Her little black dress left nothing much to the imagination, yet also was somehow very demure. The draped neckline showed the top of her swell of breasts, while the dress wrapped her torso like a second skin. Her legs were sleek and sexy below the hem, ending in stunning stiletto heels. Her hair was styled in a subdued manner, her normally tousled curls smoothed and caressing the perfect bone structure of her face.

He took a deep breath. "Wow." He held out his hands, smiling as she slipped her hands in his. "Love, you are breathtaking. Absolutely breathtaking."

Her expression showed her delight. "Thank you. You too."

Stepping into the hallway, he pulled her into his arms, and leaned down to kiss her—showing just how much he wanted her. He smiled as she returned it with equal fervor.

Pulling back, she smoothed his shirt where her fingers had grasped it so tightly. She tried to get her wits back about her. "Luther wants to say hi, he's in the living room."

"Lead the way." As she turned, and he saw her bare back, his voice sounded even deeper. "Jesus." He tried to make a joke. "And then I need a really cold shower."

She laughed, giving him a flirtatious look over her shoulder. "Yeah, yeah, yeah."

In the living room, Luther stood and give James a hug. "Good to see you, son." He gestured at Delaney. "Doesn't Lulu look like a princess?"

She rolled her eyes. "Knock it off."

James put his arm around her, pulling her close. "She does."

Pulling his phone out, Luther gestured for them to move back. "I'm taking a picture of the two of you, no arguing."

James looked down at Delaney, delighted by the idea. "No arguing from me as long as you send it to me, too."

Ten minutes later, James grinned at Delaney as she buckled herself into the passenger seat of his car while he stood by her still-open door. "Damn, sweetie."

"What?"

James got in the car, turning to her as he buckled up. He kissed her gently. "Thank you for doing this. And you do look absolutely breathtaking." His voice grew silky. "You won't wander off, right? Promise?"

"I promise."

Two hours later, Delaney realized it had been a complete whirlwind. She'd met all of James' brothers—they were partners with him in the law firm—and their wives as well. Thankfully, as it was so crowded, she didn't feel like she needed to remember names right now, with the exception of

Pam's boyfriend. The funny thing was that she'd met Thomas, but hadn't seen Pam yet, as she'd wandered off to talk to a prospective interviewee. She'd met James' father, and liked the older man immediately.

She'd just finished her second glass of champagne—sipping it slowly since she'd had almost nothing to eat all day—when she realized how much she needed to use the bathroom. Delaney handed a passing waiter her empty glass, then turned to James who was talking to one of the senior partners. She mouthed, "Ladies' room."

In the ladies' room, Delaney went to the bathroom, then stood in front of the mirror, rubbing a tiny bit of lipstick off the corner of her mouth. Just as she was about to leave, Pam walked in and exclaimed, "There you are, Laney! I was trying to find you, then when you weren't with James, I assumed I would find you here. Hold on a couple minutes, and then we can find them together, okay."

"Sounds good." While Pam was in the stall, Delaney fluffed her hair.

Pam came out and washed her hands, checked her makeup, added a touch more lipstick, then turned to her friend. "Laney, you are gorgeous. You're just plain spectacular."

Delaney was touched. "Thanks, Pammy." Her voice became more serious. "You too, as always."

"And look at us, dating two stupendous brothers." She linked her arm through Delaney's. "Who knows, maybe we'll end up sisters-in-law."

Delaney was shocked. "Seriously, you? Ms. I'm-Never-Getting-Married?"

"That was before Thomas."

Still mulling that over, Delaney opened the door to the hallway and walked out, Pam chattering behind her. As they stepped back into the ballroom, Delaney felt her blood run cold, but before she could say anything, Pam hissed, "Well, if it isn't Fuckhead."

"Pam, shhhh! Don't, not here!"

Pam started toward the well-dressed blond man talking to James' father, Delaney struggling to keep up with her long legs, especially in such high heels. Her voice was pleading as she tried to not draw attention to them. "Pam, don't! Please, Pam, please!"

Just then, Pam stopped short next to James' father, giving him a warm smile as she stretched up to kiss his cheek. "Robert."

"Pam! So good to see you. I just asked my son where you were." He looked behind Pam, "And Delaney! So wonderful to have the two of you here." He then turned to his companions, and Delaney could now see the stunning brunette in the bright red dress standing beside the focus of Pam's ire. "Do you both know Tom Duncan?"

Pam smiled sweetly. "Oh, we know the fuckhead."

The older man was shocked. Delaney jumped in, "Sorry to interrupt, sir. Yes, we know Tom, and please forgive us, we were just going to go find your sons."

Tom's eyes narrowed as he looked at Pam. "Pam, always such a pleasure." His eyes softened, as he looked appreciatively at Delaney, his gaze slowly taking in every inch of her, making her skin crawl. "Laney, so good to see you."

Laney swallowed, desperate to get away from the situation. "Tom."

Delaney looked at the older man, who was clearly confused. She felt the need to explain. "Robert, I apologize for intruding. Tom is my ex-husband, and he and Pam, well..."

Pam's eyes narrowed. "And she's my best friend, and he is the spawn of Satan."

Just then a strong, warm arm wrapped around Delaney, one hand coming to rest possessively on her lower abdomen. "There you are, love. I was getting lonely."

Delaney almost sagged in relief, feeling the safety of James's touch. His voice became cold. "Tom."

Tom looked stunned. "James. I didn't realize you and Delaney..."

James' brother came over and took Pam's hand. "Did I miss something?"

Pam kissed his cheek. "No, darling."

James looked at Tom again, his posture clearly hostile. "Yes, we're very happy, thank you."

Tom smiled somewhat wistfully. "You're a lucky man."

"Don't I know it."

Chapter Twenty-two

After the encounter, James watched in concern as Delaney withdrew from the conversations, just sitting quietly, nodding occasionally as if trying to pretend she was listening. The dinner dishes had been removed, as the waitstaff prepared to serve the decadent dessert. James leaned over and kissed Delaney's bare shoulder. "Come with me."

It was an order, not a request. Delaney stood and silently followed him out onto the mostly deserted patio. Once they were completely alone, he pulled her into his arms, and smiled slightly when he felt her sag against him. "So, are we letting a scumbag ruin our evening?"

She shook her head, not saying a word. His tone was patient. "Laney, please talk to me."

She shrugged. "There's really nothing to say. I just didn't know he'd be here. And it's not like we don't run into each other occasionally, but this was a shock. I was in my own happy zone being with you, and I wasn't prepared to see him."

"I'm so sorry, Laney."

"It's not your fault. You don't need to look at the guest list to make sure I won't freak out. Then…"

"Then?"

"Then Pam stormed over and called him a fuckhead in front of your dad."

"I caught the 'spawn of Satan' comment." He laughed outright. "Okay, I'm getting to like her more and more."

Delaney tried to shove him. "Not funny. It was embarrassing as hell. What will your father think?"

"Yes, it *is* funny. And knowing how my dad feels about fidelity and monogamy, he'd call him a fuckhead too."

Delaney was silent, leaning against him, listening to the reassuring beat of his heart. He didn't say a word, sensing her need to just be for a few minutes, but then said gently, "Is there more?"

She nodded, and whispered, "Yes."

"Tell me."

She shook her head. "I can't."

"Yes, you can. You can tell me anything."

She swallowed. "When I was married to Tom, I did everything I knew how to keep his interest. I mean, I know I'm not a beauty queen like my mom was, but no matter what I did, he fooled around with every intern who worked for his firm while we were together, then he left me for Sabrina. I know it shouldn't bother me but seeing her still makes me insecure." She closed her eyes. "Sorry, that sounded really needy."

"First, you don't sound needy. You're being honest, which I appreciate." He hugged her. "His loss, not yours." James filed away that little bit of information about her mom. "You know how beautiful you are, don't you, Laney?"

She didn't answer, so he continued, "Love, you are beautiful inside and out. He's an ass. Anyone who knows him, knows that."

Her continued silence worried him. With a firm but gentle hand, he pushed up her chin so he could see her face. "Laney, his loss. He was the fuckhead, Pam is right. Anyone who would let you get away is an idiot." He brushed away the lone tear that started to roll down her cheek, "Don't cry, love." His voice was strong. "I'm not an idiot. I'm not letting you get away. I will never cheat on you. I will never lie to you, and I'm absolutely crazy about you."

He could see hope returning to her eyes. "Really?"

"Really."

She ran her hand softly down the side of his face. "The same."

He knew what she meant, but he insisted, "Say it."

"I will never lie to you, I will never cheat on you, and yes," —she grinned like a child— "yes, I'm absolutely crazy about you."

He pulled her closer, their bodies pressed against each other, and he kissed her. Her arms went around his neck, and in her heels, they were much closer in height. It was all he could do to keep his head enough to not slide his hands down her bare back.

She pulled back to gaze adoringly at him. "Crazy about me?"

He rubbed his nose against hers. "Crazy. Absolutely crazy. All I can think about crazy." Her smile was getting wider and wider. "All I want to do is be with you, hear your voice, hold your hand crazy."

She whispered, "Me too."

Just then they heard a voice from the doorway to the ballroom. "James? You out here? Speeches are about to start."

Delaney looked up at him, smiling wistfully. "We need to go back in."

"We do." As Delaney started inside, holding his hand, he stopped and pulled her back, "Wait." He looked down at her, took her chin in his hand so that they were looking directly at each other. "I love you, Laney, I love you. Period. I don't want to keep the words in my head because it feels like it's too soon to say it. I love you; and I'm in love with you."

Her eyes widened with shock. Then she stood on her tiptoes and hugged him as tightly as she could. "I love you too. Period."

He kissed her, so thrilled and relieved to have said it. With a sigh, he pulled back. "Okay, let's go back in there and listen to the damn speeches, then get out of here."

"My thoughts exactly."

Chapter Twenty-three

As the speeches droned on, Delaney weighed her options. She knew what she'd planned tonight. Was it still the best option? Would he think it was just because he'd used the l-word? Who cared? She knew what she wanted.

She leaned closer so that she could whisper in his ear. "I have an idea."

He looked at her. "I'm listening."

Her look was mischievous again, but her tone was innocent. The heat of her breath in his ear was almost more than he could stand. "I think it's too far for you to drive me home tonight. How about you invite me for a sleepover?"

As he pulled back slightly, he could see the color rushing to her cheeks. "A sleepover?"

"Uh-huh."

His voice was like silk on her skin. "You want to sleep? In my guest room?"

She knew a challenge when she heard it. "No."

He turned so he could look at her more fully. "Then what do you want?"

Just then a burst of applause signaled the end of the speeches. She kissed him quickly. "I'll tell you at the car."

After trying to not be obviously rude as they said their goodbyes, the two of them hurriedly escaped. James pressed her against the car, leaning down to kiss the side of her neck. "You were saying?"

Her look was pure heat. "I was saying that I'd like to spend the night with you."

"And?"

Her lips were almost touching his. "What I want is to go to your place, sit by the ocean and watch the moon rise with a bottle of champagne, then go inside, take off all our clothes, and I want to touch and taste every inch of you."

For a moment, he held onto his honor. "Are you sure?"

"I'm sure." She pulled him closer by his tie. "I'm so sure that I brought a change of clothes with me in the bag I put in the backseat." She looked up at him, her eyes suddenly showing her nervousness. "If that's okay with you."

His hands were almost rough as he pulled her close. "Is that *okay*? Jesus, Laney, I've done everything I could tonight to not throw you over my shoulder and find a quiet room. I love you, and Jesus, I want you more than I can tell you." He kissed her, almost branding her. "All I want is to make love to you."

"Then let's go."

Chapter Twenty-four

At his house, he opened the car door and looked at her as he held out his hand. "You really made this decision earlier?"

She nodded. "I did. I packed a change of clothes because I wasn't going home tomorrow in this dress, and besides, if I didn't come home at all tonight without giving him notice, Luther would call out the state police."

"So, Luther knew you were spending the night before me?" His tone was menacing, but his eyes were amused.

"He did."

Without warning, he scooped her up, shifting her over his shoulder. "That's it. Not only do I not know you're ready to spend the night, but Luther knew *first*." He strode toward the door of the house, not stopping to put her down until they were in the kitchen, then, he held her as she slid down his body to stand in front of him. "I will get you for that, you know."

"I'm looking forward to it."

His tone became more serious as he traced the side of her face with one finger. "I love you, Laney. I am so glad you came into my life."

"Me too."

After Delaney slipped out of her heels, and James removed his suit coat and tie, he grabbed a bottle of champagne while she went for two glasses. Holding hands, they walked outside to the chairs overlooking the ocean. As Delaney moved to pull a chair next to his, he smiled. "We don't need two chairs. Come sit with me and I can keep you warm too."

Snuggled on his lap, Laney felt the warmth and safety of his love. He poured the champagne, and once he'd put the bottle down, he raised his glass. "To us."

"To us." She took a sip, then looked at him solemnly. "Thank you for falling in love with me."

"Likewise."

In the stillness they watched the waves in the moonlight, and when the champagne was almost gone Delaney twisted on his lap, wrapping her arms around his neck and kissing him briefly. "Would you please take me to bed now?"

"Absolutely." Holding out his hand, he smiled as she slipped her hand in his, and followed behind him almost soundlessly in her bare feet to his bedroom. The room was lit only by the moonlight streaming through the windows. He turned on the stereo which filled the room with soft piano music and turned to her. "You're sure."

"I'm sure." She turned. "Would you please unzip me?"

"Not yet." He stood in front of her. "Birth control?"

"Monthly injections, all set." She reached up to unbutton the second button on his shirt. "Health history is clean."

"Likewise." He snagged her wandering hand and kissed it. "Do you want me to use a condom?"

She was touched by his question. "No, I don't. I just want you."

"Okay." He smiled. "Then come over here for a moment." He led her over by the wingback chair she'd admired the first time and she was surprised when he sat down facing her. "So, I'm not ready to get you out of that dress yet, because I've spent all evening wanting to do this." His looked was devilish. "And since I told you I was going to get you back, you have to stay relatively still…" His long fingers stroked down the straps on her dress, barely skimming her sensitive skin. He then followed the lines of the wrappings around her waist and torso, coming close to her breasts but not touching them, making Delaney want to scream in frustration. "Turn around." When she turned, he traced the scooped line of the back of her dress, and she could feel heat flooding her. "It didn't escape my notice that in this dress there's no possible way you could be wearing a bra."

Her voice was strained. "Very observant."

She felt his fingers reach the top of the zipper where it rested just inches above her waist, and slowly start to slide it down. She trembled as his fingers skimmed her bare skin. When the zipper was done, he said quietly, "Turn around." He paused. "Please."

Delaney turned, and the look of pure desire and love on his face made tears well up in her eyes. No man had ever looked at her that way.

He saw her tears, and stood up quickly, wrapping her in his arms. "Laney! Love, if this is going too far, tell me."

Wiggling so that she could free her arms, she reached up to capture his face in her hands. "James!" She swiped away the tears. "Hello! I wasn't tearing up because I was sad, it was because I looked at you, and I could see how much you want me. It made me really happy, and sometimes when I get happy, I get teary." She kissed him, smiling when he pulled her even closer and she could feel his manhood pressing against her. Without breaking the kiss, she started unbuttoning his shirt and tugging it free of his pants. Stepping back a tiny bit, she looked at him sternly. "But so help me God, if you don't get me naked soon, with you beside me, I'm going to lose my mind."

With a swift kiss, he then dropped his shirt to the floor, and for the first time, Delaney could see the rippled muscles of his chest. With a happy sound, she reached out to run her hands down his chest, loving the feeling of his skin under her fingertips. He unbuckled his pants, but before dropping them, he reached out and snagged one of the shoulder straps of her dress. "I think I was supposed to get you out of this, right?" With that, he tugged at it, and her dress dropped to the floor, leaving her in only her small black panties. With a growl that made another rush of heat flow through her, he grasped her waist in his two hands, amazed by her beauty. He knelt down, still holding her, and kissed the shadow between her breasts reverently. "Jesus, Laney, you are the most beautiful woman I've ever seen." He traced the swells of her breasts with one finger, seeing her shiver, and watching in delight as her nipples tightened even more. Clearly, she was as impacted by his touch as he was by touching her.

"Thank you." Her voice was husky. "Can you please take me to bed now?"

Stopping just long enough to drop his pants to the floor, he led her to the bed, throwing back the duvet. He sat on the edge of the bed, clad only in his boxer briefs. With loving hands, he stroked down her sides until his fingers reached the little wisps of lace on her hips. "We don't need these." He tugged them down, smiling as she stepped out of them, kicking them to the side.

She raised one eyebrow, looking at him. "And yours?"

He stood swiftly and pushed down one side of the waistband while she pulled down on the other side.

Finally, he stood naked before her, and for a moment, Delaney couldn't believe that this absolutely gorgeous man was hers. His body was even better than she had imagined, and she couldn't wait to touch every bit of it.

Delaney climbed onto the bed, kneeling in the center, facing James. The bed shifted as he joined her, and he took her face in his hands, kissing her reverently. Gently, he pushed her down, so that she was lying on her back. Rolling onto his side, he rested his head on his hand. "I need to touch you."

She chuckled. "God, I hope so."

Slowly, he ran one hand down from her face, over her shoulders, brushing against her breasts with the palm of his hand, smiling as she arched her back to press closer to his hand. Skimming his hand down her abdomen, he could see her anticipating his touch at the junction of her thighs, but instead he slid his hand first along one leg then the other, coming close to the blonde curls, but not touching them. The second time he did this, she whimpered, and at the sound his hand stopped, mere inches from where he knew she wanted him to touch. "Getting impatient, aren't you?"

"James, enough. Please." Her voice was pleading.

Moving quickly, he covered her body with his, pressing her down into the mattress, his hard length pressed between them. He could feel her move, opening herself to him. He gazed into her eyes and leaned down to tug on her lower lip with his teeth. "I don't think so, love. I'm just getting started."

"James!" She moved, desperately trying to touch him.

"Uh-uh, Laney. Patience."

"We've been patient! Enough, now!"

He leaned back so that as he knelt over her, his legs pinned hers together. He could see her looking longingly at his manhood, and it took every ounce of his reserve to not give in and slide inside her. Clearly, she was as ready as he was, but first, he needed to truly make her his own.

"I want that too, but first, I need to do this." He leaned down and ran the tip of his tongue around each of her breasts, stopping just short of touching her nipples. Finally, when she thought she would lose her mind with the need to feel his mouth on them, he took one, then the other nipple in his mouth, gently licking them with the tip of his tongue, then sucking on each of them. Laney's delighted cry filled him with even more desire, and he had to force himself to not just stay there, sucking one then the other over and over. He moved further down her legs as he ran his tongue down her flat stomach, then stopped just before his tongue could touch those curls. His voice was silky. "I think you wanted me to touch here a while ago? Right, that was what you wanted?"

"Damn it, James. Yes! That's what I want."

He took one hand, and placed it firmly over her mound of curls, and with the touch, he felt her body rear up, and he knew how close she was to what would be her first orgasm tonight. "You like that?"

"Yes, I like that! Please James!"

"Please what?"

"I want you inside me. Please."

He moved so that he could kneel inside her legs, and as he pushed her legs apart, he could see how ready she was for him. "Not yet."

He moved closer, blowing softly on those curls. With gentle but insistent fingers, he separated her lips, and he could see how hot and wet she was. "Jesus, Laney, you are the sexiest woman on earth." He moved closer, and blew again on her exposed nub, smiling when her hips rose, as if begging for him to touch her there. With a growl, he ran his tongue around it, holding her hips still as she tried to press him even closer. Then, he slid his tongue down, and inside her, mimicking what he would soon be doing when he was finally inside her. Feeling her muscles beginning to clench, he knew she was close to her release, and he moved again so he could tug on her nub with his teeth, running his tongue around it. Feeling her hands come to his head, pushing his mouth closer, he knew she could feel the pressure building inside of her.

Hating to stop even for a second, he lifted his head just a bit, and smiled as she whimpered with the loss of his mouth. "Come, Laney. Come in my mouth. Let me taste you, please." With that plea, he once again ran his tongue down and around, just in time to feel her body clench, then flood his mouth with her honey.

She was still trembling with the strength of her orgasm when she felt him shift, moving so that she opened her legs even wider for him, and she felt the head of his manhood pressing against her. Reaching up, she put her hands on his hips, and urged him into her. When he finally was completely inside her, she looked up at him in wonder. "Please. I need you."

"My pleasure." James tried hard to restrain his urge to take her hard, wanting to forever banish any thoughts of other men. He tried to go slowly, somewhat gently, wanting to make it last for her too.

Her voice was sharp. "James!"

"Yes?"

"Hard, fast, now. We have the rest of our lives to savor, but right now, I need you." She paused, then whispered, "I need you to take me now. Please."

James had never experienced a rush of desire as strong as the one that engulfed him with her words. Holding tight to her, he honored her wishes, savoring every single feeling as he surged into her over and over. With a shout, he spilled into her, and felt her spasm around him.

Long minutes later he stirred, realizing that in his own release, he had collapsed down on her, holding her as tightly as he could. Bracing himself on an elbow, he kissed her reddened lips, which smiled with his touch. "Need to breathe?"

"Nah." She tightened her arms around him. "I can breathe just fine."

Slowly, he withdrew from her, feeling his own body reeling from the intensity of his release. Was it because he'd been waiting for so long to finally make love with her? Was that why it was so intense? Or was it their chemistry? As he rolled onto his back, he pulled her with him, keeping his arm around her. He kissed her temple. "You may be the death of me."

She wiggled slightly, so that she could brace herself on her arm. "Right back at you." She reached out and gave a gentle pinch to his nipple. "And you, you think what you did was fair?" She ran her fingers down his chest. "You made me beg."

He laughed. "No, I didn't make you beg. Just plead a little bit." A possessive hand on her hip gave a gentle squeeze. "I will make you beg; I promise you that, but not tonight." He rolled onto his side, so he could look at her. "You know I love you?"

"I do." Her look was serious. "And I love you."

"I know you do." He grinned, and Laney could see the bad boy look in his eyes. "And aren't you full of surprises? You planned to spend the night and didn't even tell me ahead of time." He tipped his head. "If I'd known, I would've had candles and roses for you."

"That was the point. I don't need candles and roses." She ran her fingers down his face. "I need you. That's it. I knew if we made a big deal ahead of time, it was going to get to be too much. This was just perfect."

Just then her stomach growled, and while they both tried to keep from laughing, within seconds, they gave into the amusement. James stood up, and for a moment, Delaney just enjoyed being able to stare at his naked body. God, he was beautiful!

He walked to the nearby closet and came back with a white t-shirt. "Come on, put this on so you don't freeze, and let's go find food."

"I'm fine."

He leaned over the bed and pulled her by the hand. "No, you aren't. You ate two bites of nothing at dinner, because of Fuckhead. Now," he said, grinning wolfishly, "if I am going to keep enjoying your body, I need to make sure you don't fade away from starvation."

With a giggle, she sat up and pulled on his shirt. When she stood, it reached almost to her knees. James pulled on pajama bottoms and turned around. He swallowed. "Shit. That is the single sexiest thing I've seen you wear, and that counts that amazing dress tonight."

She twirled around. "Thank you."

Sitting at the kitchen counter, Delaney had to admit that the turkey sandwich was delicious. "Thank you for making me dinner."

James took his last bite and grinned at her. "My pleasure."

In the bedroom, after brushing her teeth, Delaney climbed into bed still wearing his shirt. James closed the curtains, plunging the room into complete darkness. Sliding in beside her, he pulled the duvet up over them, and Delaney stretched contentedly before she reached over to kiss him.

The kiss was meant to convey good night, but it deepened quickly. His hands slipped under the shirt, as her hands went to push his pajama pants down his legs. Within minutes, he rolled on top of her, kissing her deeply. "This time, slow and long."

True to his word, it was slow and sweet, punctuated by phrases of endearment. When they reached their release together, it was just as powerful as the first time.

As she fell asleep, Delaney's last thoughts were a prayer that she wouldn't dream of cornfields that night...

Chapter Twenty-five

On Sunday morning, Delaney stood in the bathroom, checking her makeup one more time. James sat in the chair by the window, not wanting to rush her. He glanced at his watch. "Laney, ready?"

"Almost."

He stood up and walked over to the open door, smiling at the sight of her simple dress, strappy sandals, and a bright scarf tied around her neck. He leaned against the door frame, watching her, fascinated by her absolute focus on her own image. As she touched up her mascara, she griped, "Stop watching me. You'll make me poke myself in the eye."

"You look perfect. Stop fussing and let's go."

"Stop it! I'm almost ready, but don't rush me."

As she finally left the sink, she found him blocking her way. He held out his hand, and she took it, looking slightly skeptical. "What?"

"You are absolutely stunning, and you don't even know it."

As they pulled out of his driveway, he looked over at her briefly, seeing her eyes were already hidden by her sunglasses, making him feel at a disadvantage as to how she was really feeling. "I hate that we're doing this and then I'm dropping you off at your place. I'd much rather have you stay over again tonight."

She squeezed his hand quickly. "Hello! At some point before I go back to work tomorrow, I need to get at least a couple hours of sleep."

"Are you saying that you don't sleep at my house?"

She laughed. "I'm saying that I absolutely love staying with you, but occasionally, we both need to get more than two or three hours of sleep."

"Just because one of us"—he nudged her leg— "can't keep her hands to herself…"

"True." She looked out the window at the passing scenery, trying to relax. "Tell me again who's going to be there."

He could feel her anxiety over the luncheon. "You've met most of them already. My parents will be there, my four brothers, Pam, my three sisters-in-law—including Denise, who you know. I think all my nieces and nephews will be there. As of right now, there are seven of them, but one more is on the way. Mom will have made an obscene amount of food, it'll be a cookout, the kids will run around like wild animals. Usually some of us end up playing either football or ultimate frisbee. It's just a time to get together." He tried to understand her obvious nerves. "Did you have family events like this before your parents died?"

Her voice sounded far away. "Sort of. I only had a few relatives, but I do remember some family get-togethers."

He didn't want to lose her in painful memories. "Anyway, my mom adores you, and my dad can't wait to get to know you better. You've met my brothers, and you have Pam and Denise to protect you when they decide to grill you. It'll be fun, I promise." Just then he signaled to pull into a long driveway, and Laney tried to not be overwhelmed by the property. When he stopped the car, he turned to her, pulling off her sunglasses so he could see her eyes. "Laney, listen to me. After lunch, if you're ready to go, just say so. I'll take you whenever you want."

"Thank you."

As they walked up the front steps, Laney could hear small children yelling inside. As he reached for the doorknob, he stopped, turned, and kissed her hard. "Love you."

"Love you."

Tomorrow and Yesterday

Chapter Twenty-six

The party had been in swing for quite some time when James realized that he hadn't seen Delaney in a while. After a raucous lunch, the group had split up. He'd gone to play football with his brothers and some of his nieces and nephews. Laney had watched for a while, but then disappeared.

Striding into the kitchen, he smiled seeing his mother supervising one of her granddaughters as the child frosted cupcakes. He snagged an unfrosted one off the tray. "Thank you!"

His mother swatted him. "You never change!"

"And that makes you happy." He looked around the kitchen, expecting that Laney might have joined his mother. "Have you seen Delaney?"

She shook her head, keeping an eye on the child. "No, I haven't seen her in a while. Last time was when she was headed outside with Devon."

"Devon?" His heart sank. Of all the grandchildren in the family, five-year-old Devon was the most difficult. Behind closed doors, the rest of the family discussed that he might be on the autism spectrum, but his parents wouldn't consider this, and because of it, Devon's behaviors were getting more and more extreme, and everyone worried about him.

Just then Robert strode into the kitchen, and grabbed a frosted cupcake, moving before his wife could swat him. "They're down at the shore."

James was surprised. "They are?"

"Yeah. Last I saw, they were headed down the path with Devon talking a mile a minute to her."

Walking slowly down to the beach, he wondered how Delaney had gotten roped into taking the wild child.

At the beach, he looked for them, and finally spotted Delaney sitting on the sand, leaning against a rock. As he came closer, he realized that his nephew was sitting next to her, as close as he could, and together they were making a design in the sand with a pile of shells.

Delaney heard him approaching and looked up. Her voice was soft. "Devon, look, Uncle James came to see our project."

James braced for him to jump wildly or to shout at him, but instead, the little boy looked up and said, "Hi, Uncle James. Want to help us?"

"I'd love to."

Sitting on the sand next to him, James looked at the design. They had used pieces of sea glass and shells to make a scene of an octopus in the waves. He smiled. "What a great picture!"

Laney put her arm around the little boy and hugged him. "It was Devon's idea. I just helped gather the materials. He's an artist, just like you."

James looked at the little boy with interest. "Dev, do you like to draw?"

"I love to. Sometimes my teacher gets mad because I draw in school when I'm supposed to be learning." He shrugged. "I can listen better that way when she talks. I just like to draw."

James had never known his nephew liked to draw. "Wow. I was like that too."

An hour later, James sat down in one of the Adirondack chairs, and smiled as Delaney walked by. Grabbing her wrist, he pulled her to sit down in the chair with him. "Hi. Come sit with me."

She sat down, wrapping one arm around his neck and kissing his cheek. "Hi."

"Having fun?"

She nodded at him, smiling. "It's been a great day. Thank you."

Just then a small body crashed into them, and before James knew what was happening, Devon had wiggled his way onto both of their laps. "I want to sit with you too."

James had to laugh as he watched the little boy snuggle into Delaney, clearly feeling safe and special with her. As the family visited, James was shocked to see how calm Devon was, and how appropriate he was during the conversation. When he started to interrupt at one point, before any other adult could scold him, Delaney whispered, "We take turns, remember. Your turn next." And the little boy waited until there was an opening in the conversation to speak.

When it was time to go, James hid a smile as he watched every member of his family hug Delaney good-bye. Clearly, they all loved her, and it made him so happy to see how relaxed she looked with them. He had known they would take to her.

They were just about to go out the front door when there was a loud screech. As James turned, he saw Devon running full out, screaming, "*Laney*!!"

Delaney moved quickly in front of James, and as he watched in amazement, she crouched down, bracing herself for the impact of his small body. Even braced, the force almost knocked her over.

The little boy was clearly distraught. "You were leaving, and you didn't give me a hug!" As he said this, he wrapped his arms around her neck convulsively.

She hugged him, sitting down on the ground, and rocked him. "Dev, my friend, you're right. I am so sorry."

He continued to hold onto her, so his words were muffled. "And you're my best friend, and you're leaving."

She smiled and kissed his head. "My friend, I will see you again soon, I promise." She hugged him. "Look at me, buddy."

His tear-filled eyes looked up at her. She rested her forehead against his. "I asked your mommy and daddy if you and I could go get ice cream soon. They said yes, and I'm going to call your mom tomorrow to find a time to do it, okay? It may take up to ten big sleeps to see each other again, but I promise, we will."

"You promise?"

She held out her hand, her pinky crooked. "Pinky swear."

In the car, James pulled out onto the road before saying, "You have quite an admirer."

"It's a mutual thing. He's awesome."

James laughed. "You know you are the only one, including his parents, who say that, right? Most of the time people are gritting their teeth around him." He paused, looking at her briefly as he stopped at a stop sign. "Although, sitting on the beach with you, and then again when he sat with us in the chair, *that* was a different kid."

"Maybe I'm the first person in his life in a while who didn't have preconceived notions about him." She stretched her arms in front of her. "And this is what I do. I have a dozen Devons at any one time at work."

"Shoulder still bothering you?" As she nodded, he said, "I hadn't thought about that. He's unusual in our family, so probably we aren't terribly tolerant."

"Want to go get ice cream with us?"

"Of course I do!" He took the exit ramp for her street. "Want me to fix your shoulder?"

She reached out to squeeze his hand. "I would love you to, but no. I love you, you love me, and frankly, your fingers get anywhere near my shoulder, and we are going to be naked, and as much as I want that, I really do need to make sure I'm ready for tomorrow."

Before he could feel rejected, she grinned cheekily. "And I have a board meeting tomorrow night, but I'd like to invite you for a sleepover on Tuesday. I'll make dinner, and you can fix my shoulder however you like."

"A sleepover?"

"Well, maybe a little-bit-of-*sleep*-over."

"I'll be there."

Chapter Twenty-seven

Weeks later, Delaney stood in her closet, looking for something comfortable to wear in the heat, holding the phone to her ear as she shuffled clothes on the rack. "I know. But tomorrow night I'll be there, I promise."

He grumbled. "And you'll behave?"

Delaney pulled a blouse off a hanger, tossing it through the open door to her bed. "I'm going to a bachelorette party with friends from college. We're all professional, adult women now. Any wild days we had are long behind us. Yes, I'll behave."

"And if you have too much to drink, you'll call me to come get you?"

"James! You're going to dinner with your brother, remember? You're more likely to drink more than me with him anyway. Pam is with me, I'm driving, we'll be fine."

"Promise me."

She sighed, torn between being touched by his concern, and irritated by his controlling nature. "I promise. If I have too much to drink, I'll either Uber home or call you."

"Me, not Uber."

"Fine!" She tried to soften her tone. "I'll be home by nine and will text you then to see if you're home."

Delaney realized that her phone had buzzed in her pocket. She saw a text: *You said you'd be home by nine. It's 10:30 now – are you okay and do you need me to come get you?*

For a split second, Delaney felt like she was being scolded, then felt the warmth of his love and concern. She typed: *All goo will head home son.*

Her phone buzzed again almost immediately. *You will stay there, and I will come get you. When do you want me to be there?*

Completely irritated, Delaney moved into a guest room, and hit speed dial. "You don't need to come get me!"

His tone was annoyingly calm. "You just sent me a text with two spelling mistakes in it. You've never sent one, not one, in all the texts you've sent me. At the very least, you're buzzed. You aren't driving home, you aren't calling an Uber, I will come get you and either bring you here or to your house. This is not a discussion; this is what we are doing. I love you, you love me, and I can't take the idea of you driving or getting in a car with a stranger right now."

"Fine! Then come get me." Even to her own ears, Delaney knew her tone was petulant.

"When?"

"What do you mean when?"

"Delaney! When do you want me to come get you? I can leave the house now, and be there in about fifteen minutes, or I can leave later, when you want. You tell me." He took a deep breath. "I'm not trying to take you from your friends, I'm just asking when you want me to get there."

Delaney leaned her head against the wall, realizing that she was feeling tipsy at the very least. "An hour. Can you be here in an hour?"

"I can." Standing in his kitchen, he rubbed his forehead. "Promise me you'll stay put. I'll be there in an hour. If you want to stay longer, fine, I can wait outside. But promise me you'll stay there."

"I promise." Her voice dipped. "I'm sorry I'm being a pain."

"Sweetheart, you aren't being a pain. Just stay there, have fun, and I'll be there in an hour."

"I promise." Delaney sat down on the edge of a nearby chair. "Thank you."

"You're welcome. I'll see you in a bit. Love you."

"Love you."

Another glass of champagne in her, Delaney secretly was glad when her phone buzzed in her pocket exactly one hour later. *I'm here. I can wait as long as you want.*

He smiled when she responded, *Saying goodbye, be RT.*

Two minutes later, Delaney opened the car door, and sank thankfully into the seat. "Hi."

"Hi." He smiled at her. "Are you going to put on the seatbelt, or do you need help?"

"I can do it." She buckled herself in and looked at him tiredly. "Please get me out of here."

"My pleasure. Where to?" James put the car in gear, but didn't step on the gas, waiting for her answer. Delaney looked at him as if she hadn't heard the question. "Laney? Where to?"

She stared at him, chewing on her lower lip. "Laney?"

"Your house." She looked directly at him, and he could see her troubled eyes. "We need to talk, then…I don't know…if you want I can sleep in the guest room."

James looked at her in confusion. "Okay, my house. You want to talk. We'll worry about the rest later."

"Okay." She closed her eyes, resting her head on the headrest. "And if I ever get near champagne or tequila again, shoot me."

At his house, he pulled into the garage, and smiled as Delaney stirred. "You're alive. I was beginning to wonder."

"I'm alive. I'll feel like shit tomorrow, but still alive."

In the kitchen, James gestured to one of the stools. "Have a seat." James walked to the fridge, pouring her a tall glass of seltzer with orange juice and handed it to her with two Advil. "Drink this."

She did as she was told. After drinking almost half of the seltzer, she looked at him leaning against the counter, watching her carefully. "Thank you, that helps."

"Good." He smiled gently. "Okay, love of mine, talk to me. What the hell happened there tonight?"

Delaney looked at him solemnly. "I think I learned too much tonight."

He realized this might be a long conversation, so he walked around the counter, pulled out a stool and sat down facing her. "Explain."

"Do you know what Promise Keepers are?"

James felt like he was in quicksand. What the hell was he supposed to say now? "Yes. Somewhat. When I was a public defender, I defended a woman who killed her Promise Keeper husband, and I did a lot of research then." He was so confused. "Why, Laney? You went to a bridal event. Lily certainly isn't going to sign a Promise Keeper contract. What the hell triggered this?"

She seemed lost in her own memories. "After my parents died, I lived with two separate Promise Keeping couples, foster families. They taught Promise Keeping in schools as part of health class. My father often said he and my mother should have signed the Promise Keepers' contract. It's not that I thought being a Promise Keeper was what I wanted, but it limited the scope of what I thought about relationships and sex."

"Okay." *Where was she going with this?*

"Tonight, as Lily got her gifts, we were drinking, and they were talking about things…" Her face was bright red. "They were talking about things…" she repeated, jumping off the stool. "I'll be right back," she said as she ran for the bathroom.

In the bathroom, Delaney splashed cold water on her face. How could she ask him about these things? It was too embarrassing.

Just then the door opened, and Delaney protested, "I'm in here!"

"Yes, you are. And you aren't going to the bathroom, so I'm inviting myself in. What were they talking about?" As he asked, he leaned against the door frame, blocking her exit.

With a sigh, Delaney sat down on the closed toilet seat, and looked down at her feet. "They were talking about sex."

"Of course they were. It was a bridal event. Guys talk about sex at bachelor parties. It's what people do."

"No, they were talking specifics…" She was too agitated to say more.

"Laney, help me out here. I've seen, touched, tasted every inch of you, like you have me. What were they talking about that bothered you that much?"

She exclaimed, "It didn't bother me! I just didn't know that, well, people like us…"

He moved so that he could pull her into his arms, sitting down on the small wooden chest by the door. "People like us do what?"

"Okay, here's the thing. I was raised to believe that sex was first for procreation, then for some release, and that most couples planned it. And that it could be fun, but it was within guidelines or rules, and tonight, they were talking about things that I've never thought about doing, or thought about whether you wanted to do them, and…" She looked up at him. "And I don't know what to do!"

Sounding perfectly calm and businesslike was probably the best way to handle this. "What things?"

"What do you mean, *what things*?"

"What things were they talking about?"

She sounded exasperated. "Spanking and tying each other up…and talking dirty. And other things, but those are the ones I remembered."

"You remember them because they sounded interesting?"

Her blush was visible even in the soft lighting of the bathroom. "James!"

"Laney, listen to me. I love what we do when we make love. I love every bit of it. And if you want to do other things, I'm interested. The only thing off the table is me hurting you. But other than that?" He nuzzled her neck, seeing her body respond even in her agitated state. "The idea of spanking you a bit, especially when you've scared me when I thought you'd be home a long time ago? Yes, I admit that spanking that perfect behind of yours once, then kissing it, yes, that turns me on. But if it wasn't a turn on for you, then forget about it. Tying you up? Only if you wanted. You tying me up? Hell, yes. Talking dirty, yes, I admit that I would find it a turn on, but again, if it wasn't for you, then I can forgo it." He turned her chin so she had to look at him. "Laney, pure and simple, you turn me on. I love to make love with you. If there is something you're willing to try, I'm game."

She rested her head on his shoulder, trying to sort through everything he'd just said. "You mean it?"

"What? That I'm game for anything? Yes. That I love you more than I can tell you, and you're the sexiest woman I've ever known? Yes."

"That you'd be interested in doing some of those things?"

"Yes. Whatever you want."

A sudden yawn racked her body. With a swift movement, James stood up, cradling her in his arms. "Okay, lovey, time for bed. We can finish this conversation in the morning."

Exhausted, she snuggled closer. "Can I still sleep with you? Even if I'm buzzed off my ass, and need to sleep this off?"

"Especially then."

Within minutes, he'd helped her into one of his t-shirts, then tucked her into bed under the soft duvet, climbing in beside her. Pulling her close, he wrapped a strong arm around her, then kissed her temple. "Good night, Laney, love you." He pulled her closer. "Thank you for talking with me about it."

She wiggled even closer. "Thank you for not thinking I was crazy."

James laid awake long after Delaney fell into an exhausted sleep. With the soft light of the moon streaming into the bedroom from the crack in the curtains, he watched her beautiful face as she slept. Pieces of information were slowly falling into place about her past. Her mother was a beauty queen. A small family, with limited family events. Her father had wanted to be a Promise Keeper. She'd lived with foster families. What was her true story?

She sighed in her sleep and snuggled closer to him. One blonde curl fell forward over one eye. Gently, James brushed it back. What did her story matter? Just looking at her, he could feel his heart constrict with his love for the enigmatic woman beside him.

Delaney woke up realizing the sun was streaming through the curtains and she was alone in the bed. She could smell coffee, so she knew James was up. Sitting up slowly, she waited to see if her head hurt, which it only did a little bit. A shower, Advil, and she would feel just fine.

In the bathroom, she smiled, seeing a note taped to the mirror. *Coffee is ready, muffins in the kitchen. I'm in the studio, come see me when you're ready—love you.*

Two Advil, a long, hot shower, and Delaney was ready for the day. Thankful that she had clothes at James' house, she dressed in jeans and a t-shirt before heading to the kitchen for coffee.

Mug in hand, she walked down the hallway to the studio, and with the door open, she could walk in and look at James without him realizing it. She stood in the doorway, seeing him dressed in faded jeans and a t-shirt that hugged his upper body like a second skin. He was working on a new painting with that absolute focus she loved to watch. She sipped her coffee, watching his arm muscles ripple as he shaded an area of the huge painting. Love surged through her, almost taking her breath away. This amazing man, so kind, so beautiful, so creative, was hers. He loved her. He loved her even when she was a drunk, emotional mess. He loved her when she was an anxious control freak. He loved her, period. And all those arm muscles rippling as he painted? She had to admit that just watching him turned her on.

His voice interrupted the beginning of her amorous thoughts. "You having fun watching me?"

She realized that he spoke without turning around. She smiled smugly. "I am." She chuckled. "How long have you known I was standing there?"

"Since you got there." He stopped painting and turned. "Sweetheart, you get anywhere near me, and I can feel your energy. I just figured that when you were ready to announce yourself, you would."

Delaney walked toward him slowly, seeing his eyes darken as she came closer. He put down his brush, as she put down her coffee cup. As her arms went up around his neck, he slid his hands under her shirt, and Delaney sighed happily. "Good morning."

He grinned as his hands slid higher, grazing the edge of her bra. "Good morning."

"So, ask me what I was thinking while I was watching you?"

"What were you thinking when you were watching me? That I am the greatest painter of all time?"

"You are to me." She stretched on her tiptoes. "I was thinking how amazing you are, and how much I love you, and how sexy you are." She kissed him briefly. "And then I was looking at your arm muscles as you painted, and I was getting so turned on."

"Really?" He moved his hands so that his thumbs could stroke the underside of her breasts, smiling as he heard her sigh happily. "You were getting turned on?"

She reached out and unbuttoned his jeans. "Uh huh. Like I need you *now* turned on."

He started to take her hand to lead her out of the studio, but she stood still. "Now. Here."

Her words inflamed his already heated blood. "As you wish." With a fluid movement, he tossed his shirt aside before removing hers, unhooking her bra and dropping it to the floor too. Shedding his jeans, he watched as she slid hers down her legs with her panties, and then she was standing naked in his studio, her skin glowing in the sunlight. She took his hand, leading him to the lounging couch his mother had insisted needed to be in his studio. "Lie down."

James laid down on the couch and watched as she pulled his boxer briefs down his legs, tossing them to the side without a glance. Kneeling over him, Delaney slid her hands down his chest, coming to rest just to the side of his straining manhood. "Damn, you are one beautiful man, James McDaniels."

He smiled, his hands resting on her hips, loving seeing the heat in her eyes. "To clarify, Delaney Adams, I am *your* man. Just yours."

At his words, Delaney moved so she was straddling him, moving slowly until he filled her fully. With sun streaming down on them through the huge windows, she moved over him, loving the sensation of having him so deeply inside her, their bodies in full and constant contact. She tried to keep the rhythm slow, but within minutes, their passion engulfed them both, and she needed to reach the release she'd been craving since she'd seen him that morning. As it hit, she felt his body clench as well, and he shouted her name as he poured into her.

Delaney collapsed down on his broad chest with a contented sigh.

His voice showed his humor. "Well, good morning to you too."

Her head was resting over his heart, listening to the comforting sound of his heartbeat. "Good morning." She kissed his chest. "I've discovered the cure for a hangover."

He laughed, rubbing her bare back. "How's your head?"

"It's fine." She chuckled. "It shouldn't be, but it is." She kissed him again. "It's because you took such good care of me. Thank you."

"My pleasure."

They lay there in silence, just enjoying being together. Delaney yawned. James kissed her temple. "Sleepy?"

"Yeah." She raised her head to look at him. "It's your fault. You working your magic made me so relaxed I'm sleepy again."

"Then why not stay right here and take a nap?"

She smiled. "That sounds like a great idea. You don't mind me being in the room while you work?"

"Of course not." He slid out from under her, making sure that he gently guided her body onto the couch. "Be right back." Naked, he strode across the room to a closet she hadn't noticed before. Within minutes, he was back with a soft blanket, which he tucked around her, leaning down to kiss her forehead. "Sleep."

"Sounds good."

Within minutes, James heard her breathing change as she fell asleep, the sun glinting off her curls. Putting down his paintbrush, he picked up his sketchbook and started to draw.

An hour later, Delaney awakened slowly, smelling the paint, knowing that James was working before she rolled over. Looking over at him, she could see the absolute focus on his canvas. "Hi again."

"Good morning again."

Delaney stood up, and for a moment, started to wrap the blanket around her naked body. Seeing the hint of a smile start on James' face, she dropped the blanket defiantly, and glared when he laughed. "Wow! Aren't you getting brave!"

"Bite me!" She stalked across the room to where her clothes were now neatly folded on a stool, and dressed, trying not to give in to the urge to try to cover her nakedness as quickly as possible.

Once dressed, Delaney looked at James, and rolled her eyes. "Okay, now I'm going to get food and more coffee. Do you want anything?"

"All set right now." He gestured at the canvas. "I'll be ready to stop pretty soon if you want to do something."

Delaney walked over and stretched up on her tiptoes to kiss him. "Paint as long as you like. I'm going to get food and deal with emails, so I can self-amuse."

After getting a muffin and another mug of coffee, Delaney settled at the kitchen counter and ate while flipping through the paper. Afterward, she took care of her dishes, and walked up the stairs to the bedroom to brush her teeth. When she got there, she stopped in shock, seeing the sketchbook on the bed. Stepping closer, she saw the words at the top of the page: *My favorite view...*

The pencil sketch showed a line drawing of Delaney asleep on the couch, sunbeams streaming over her from the huge windows. Delaney sat down on the bed, her heart constricting with the power of the love shown in that drawing.

Without thinking, Delaney dropped it on the bed, and ran down the stairs to his studio. James had heard her footsteps, and had turned, just as she ran towards him, hugging him tightly. "Thank you! I love it so much!"

Making sure to keep his brush away from her, he hugged her, and kissed her nose. "I'm glad. You won't let me sketch you when you're awake, so I have to take my opportunities when you're sleeping."

She wrapped her arms up around his neck and kissed him. "You can sketch me whenever you want. And I love that one so much." She suddenly blushed. "Can I keep it?"

He laughed and pulled her closer. "Of course you can. It's yours."

A little while later, Delaney wandered back to the studio. "James?"

"Uh huh?" His back was to her as he focused on shading on one part of the canvas.

"What are your plans for the rest of the day and evening?"

He stopped painting to turn and look at her. "I don't know. I guess I was assuming that either you were staying here, or we were going to your place—no real formal plans, just hanging out." He tipped his head. "Why?"

"Pam just messaged me. She and Thomas are going into Boston in a couple hours. She wants to go to the sales at the Prudential, then go to Ostra, and wondered if we'd like to go with them, or at least meet them there."

He put down the paintbrush to walk over to her, pulling her close so he could kiss her forehead. "Do you want to?"

She nodded slowly. "I do." She hugged him. "I like the idea of the four of us doing something."

"Me too. Sounds good." He stretched. "Let me clean up here, then grab a shower, then why don't we say we'll meet them at Thomas'?"

"Great."

The group pulled into the parking garage under the Prudential, having enjoyed a lively conversation on the way into the city. Getting out of the car, Pam checked her hair and makeup, then linked arms with Delaney. "Okay, boys. We're going shopping. You're welcome to come along, and offer your opinions, but don't get in our way."

James laughed, liking Pam more and more as he got to know her. "Understood."

Minutes later, the two men looked at each other in amusement as Pam said, "Laney! Look at that blouse. That would be perfect with your black tulip skirt."

With that, the two of them ducked into the store, leaving the men in the hallway. Thomas looked at his brother in bemusement. "What in God's name is a tulip skirt?"

"No clue. But there is no way in hell that I'm telling your woman that. She'd think I was an idiot for not knowing."

"Yeah. She can be rather scathing. That's part of her charm. She tells me when she thinks I'm a shithead, instead of acting like I'm God's gift to the world. It's refreshing and keeps me on my toes." He gestured toward a bench in the middle of the wide, bustling, hallway. "We might as well sit."

The two brothers sat, talked, and laughed, and James realized that it was truly enjoyable to hang out with his brother this way, something they'd never done before. They chatted until the two women emerged from the store, each with a large shopping bag. Delaney grinned at James, laughing. "I told you they'd still be here."

Pam kissed Thomas' cheek. "And they can carry the bags."

Over the next hour, they moved throughout the mall—the women running in and out of stores, the men usually opting to find a bench to people watch. Finally, the women returned, and Pam said, "Okay, boys. We want to go to Lord and Taylor's, then we're done, and you can buy us a drink and dinner."

Thomas grinned as he wrapped his arm around Pam, kissing her briefly. "That sounds like an offer I can't refuse. We've sat here all afternoon, then we get to buy you dinner too?"

"Absolutely."

Delaney had stopped slightly to the side of the group, wanting to tuck a couple of the receipts further down in her purse. James had noticed that she'd stopped, so he slowed down as well, but was standing a few feet away from her.

Just then a tall, willowy brunette in a short pencil skirt, white silk blouse, and gorgeous stiletto heels shouted, "James!"

Delaney watched in fascination as the woman rushed toward him, so absorbed in what was happening that she didn't see or hear Thomas say, "Oh, shit," to Pam.

James turned, just as the woman got to him and opened her arms to wrap him in a tight hug, stretching up just a tiny bit to kiss his cheek. "It's so good to see you!"

"Nicole." James tried to figure out what to do, turning toward Delaney, not realizing that the woman still had her arm around him. "Laney, this is Nicole. Nicole, Delaney."

Delaney froze, not sure what to do. This stunning woman had her man in a tight grip. Her voice sounded wobbly. "Nicole."

"Oh, hi." She completely ignored the three of them, instead focusing fully on James, reaching up to stroke his hair. "It's been so long, Jimmy. I've missed you. How have you been?"

"Fine." James took a step back, breaking the physical contact. "You?"

"Good, busy but good. We should get together to catch up."

James' brain was not working like it should. "That would be good."

She smiled. "Great. I'll be in touch." She hugged him again, hard, pressing her body against his as she kissed his cheek one more time. As she stepped back, she gave a slight wave. "Lacey, good to meet you." And she walked away.

The silence was deafening. Delaney could see that Pam wanted to go stomp the other woman, which was all she needed to make this situation worse. "Pam, you wanted to go to Lord and Taylor's, right?"

Pam saw the hurt and anger that her best friend was barely containing and knew that she was trying to get away from James right then. "I do, Laney-loo. Let's go." She held out her hand. "Come on."

Delaney took her hand, striding forward, not looking at James at all. As she walked by him, he put out his hand to try to snag her arm, shocked when she twitched away to avoid his touch. "Delaney?"

Delaney averted her eyes, her voice cold. "We're going shopping."

"Wait a minute!" When she kept walking, he tried to snag Pam's arm. "Pam?"

Pam stopped, and watched in some amusement as Delaney kept walking, but snapped over her shoulder, "I'll be in dresses, Pam."

"Be right there, Laney."

As Delaney walked away from them, James turned to Pam in complete confusion. "Why's she mad at me? What did I do?"

Pam's eyes widened. "What'd you do?" She looked at Thomas and her voice became scathing. "What did he do?"

Thomas held up his hands in a gesture of surrender. "Not getting in the middle of this one, darling. You can tell him." He grinned at her. "At least I know what he did."

By this point, James was getting mad, and had his hands on his hips. "What the hell is going on? What did I do?"

Pam's voice rose. "You *ass*! You just let a woman who you used to sleep with come up and hug you like she was ready to get naked with you. Then not once but *twice*, you let her kiss you, with her hands all over you. When you finally introduced her to Delaney you didn't say, 'This is Delaney, the love of my life.' You said it like she was the pizza delivery guy or something." She shook her head. "You are a fucking idiot. And frankly, I'd like to kick you in the balls right now." She shook her head in disgust. "I'm going to find her."

"I didn't go up to Nicole, she approached me!"

"And you didn't think you could handle it better? What, she got close enough and you were thinking with your dick? Jesus, you're an idiot!" She turned to walk away. "Tom, I'll be back in a bit."

"No!" James' voice was louder than he expected. "No. You're staying here . . . or go shopping or something. This is between us, not you. I'll go find her."

Her look was skeptical. "You ever seen her really mad?"

"No."

"Good luck, that's all I'm saying." She shook her head. "We'll be in shoes if you need us." Her voice softened a tiny bit. "She was going to look at dresses. Third floor, far side of the store."

"Thank you."

James quickly found the escalator, riding it to the third floor. Following the signs, he found the dress department, and spotted the familiar blonde curls. He walked up behind her as she flipped through a rack of dresses, several already over her arm. He put his hands on her hips, moving to kiss the back of her neck. His voice was gentle. "Hi."

She moved before he could kiss her, pulling away from his hands—her movements sharp and definitive. Completely ignoring him, she continued to flick through the dresses without saying a word.

Within seconds, James could feel his temper rising, but he tried to keep the anger out of his voice. "You aren't speaking to me?"

Without turning around, Delaney snapped, "I have nothing to say right now."

"You don't?" He sounded irritated even to his own ears. "Nothing? You have *nothing* to say?"

Delaney turned toward him, her face stony, but her voice was sickly sweet. "James, I'm going to try these dresses on right now." And she turned and walked away from him.

James tried to unclench his fists, willing his body into some sense of calm. He was trying to talk to her. Why was she being so stubborn? "Then I'm going with you, and we can talk in the dressing room."

"You aren't going in the dressing room with me!"

"Why not? They're gender neutral now. No one cares if we go in one together."

"You aren't going with me!"

"Oh yes, I am. If you won't talk to me here, then we'll talk there."

"Fine!"

In the dressing room, she hung the garments on the hook and looked at him in disgust. "Say what you want to say and get out so I can try them on."

"Say what *I* want to say? You're the one who walked away back there."

James watched as Delaney backed as far away from him in the small space as she could, her arms around herself protectively. "Really? That's what you think?"

"I do."

Her voice was incredulous as she asked, "You want to know what I want to say?"

"Yes!"

Her voice cracked and she was clearly trying to hold back tears. "What I want to say is that if she's who you want, go to her. If you care so little about me that you would let a woman act like that with you, then we aren't where we thought we were as a couple."

"Delaney! What are you talking about? A woman I used to date hugged me, that's all."

"No, that's *not* all! A woman you used to date hugged you repeatedly, kissed you twice, kept her arm around you when you introduced us, and when she said she'd like to get together, you said yes!"

"I didn't mean it. I was just surprised by the whole thing." His phone buzzed.

Delaney held out her hand. The tears were gone, and her anger was back in full force. She barked, "Give me your phone."

He thought about arguing but decided against it. Handing over the phone, Delaney flipped it over and hit the home button. As it lit up, James could see with horror that it showed a text from Nicole: *So good to see you. Love to get together in the next few days – happy to come out to the house or meet you in Providence. Let me know what works for you.*

Delaney handed the phone back to him. "And you even still have her photo on your phone, so you get a close-up of her when you hear from her." Her tone got even more sarcastic. "How nice."

"Delaney! She means nothing to me, hasn't for a long, long time. Yes, her photo is still on my phone. I will delete it right now if that's what you want. I love you. *You.* I never loved her. That's why we broke up. She loved me and kept waiting for me to fall in love with her, but it didn't happen. You? I fell in love with you on our first date. You know that." He held out his hands. "Tell me what to do to make this right. I screwed up. I was shocked seeing her, and I wasn't thinking straight. I'm sorry, Laney. Forgive me."

She saw the distress in his eyes and felt her anger dissolving. "You hurt my feelings. I felt like I didn't matter. And she called me Lacey, and you did nothing."

"I know." He smiled. "I was wrong. So wrong that Pam threatened to kick me. I'm sorry."

Delaney stepped forward; her arms still crossed. "How would you have felt if Tom ever came up and hugged me in front of you?"

His answer was almost instantaneous. "I'd kill him, or at least threaten him. I didn't like him leering at you at the party. If he'd touched you, I'd have probably hit him."

She nodded. "Exactly. You did the whole possessive male thing then, which I both understood and somewhat enjoyed."

"Then what's the problem?"

"You reacted that way when it was someone looking at *me*, but I'm supposed to be okay with a woman that I know you've slept with touching you like you're *hers*?"

Finally, he fully got why she was so upset. "No. You aren't." His eyes were sad. "I fucked up. I'm sorry, and it won't happen again. I'll send her a text ending this, block her messages and take her picture off my phone, and I will make it up to you, I promise."

"Now."

"Now, what?"

"Do it now. While we're both standing here, while I can see it. Do it now."

For a moment, James felt irritated that she was insisting on it right then, like she didn't trust him. But if this was what it would take to make it better, he made sure to be quick as he pulled out his phone and typed: *Hi Nicole, thanks for your message. I'm going to decline getting together – Delaney and I are building our lives together, so for me to get together with you would be wrong. Be well.*

He held out the phone to Delaney. "Okay?"

Her tone was dry. "You could tell her that if she ever touches you again, I'll slit her throat."

He tried to hide a smile. "Want to hit send?"

"Can I block her after?"

"Absolutely."

Within seconds, Delaney had sent the text, blocked her number and removed the photo. She handed the phone back to James. "Here."

"Better?"

Her voice was tentative. "Better. Not great. Better."

He held out his arms, relieved when she came toward him, lying her head on his chest, and not pulling away when he wrapped his arms around her. As she leaned against him, she grumbled, "You fucking ass."

"I am an ass. I'm sorry." He kissed her hair. "I'm sorry. I was wrong. You were right to be pissed."

She still sounded irritated. "And I will kill her if she touches you ever again."

"Okay."

"And my name is not Lacey!"

He chuckled. "No, it's not. It's Delaney, or Laney, or love-of-mine, or baby, or even Lulu. But not Lacey."

He could feel her start to smile where her face was pressed against him. "And if you ever think you are being funny and call me Lacey, I'll kick you."

"Fine."

Taking a step back, Delaney looked up at him, then put a hand on either side of his face. Her tone was serious. "I love you. And yes, I did just have a major attack of jealousy. And maybe I overreacted, but…"

He tightened his arms around her, pulling her closer. "But what?"

"But I love you, and suddenly this woman was touching you like you're hers, and it hurt a lot." She stroked one side of his face. "It hurt way more than I would've actually expected it to."

"Because you love me more than you realized?" He tried to keep the happiness out of his voice.

"Yes." She shoved his chest. "And don't go all smug on me."

He leaned down and kissed her lightly. "Laney, I love you more than I can tell you. And yes, this little shit show taught me too. You walked away, wouldn't talk to me, wouldn't look at me, and I was afraid, almost panicky. I need you in my life. I love you. Period. No one else. You."

"Likewise." She stretched up and kissed him.

With the touch of her lips, desire and relief coursed through him, and without realizing it, he pulled her as tightly against him as he could. Her arms wound around his neck as she kissed him back with equal fervor.

Voices outside the dressing room interrupted them, making them remember where they were. She pulled back slightly and looked at him. "We are not making love in a dressing room!"

He smiled, sliding his hands slowly up her back, seeing her eyes darken again. "Why not?"

She smacked his shoulder. "Get out and let me try on these dresses."

He shook his head. "No. I'll stay here, and you can try them on. That way I can give you my opinion."

"Fine." She raised one eyebrow. "No touching."

"You take the fun out of everything."

"Sit!" She pointed to the bench in the corner, and with a rueful grin, he sat down.

James watched in fascination as Delaney slipped out of her slacks and blouse, standing in just her underwear, before she pulled on a dark green dress. Without her asking, he stood and moved to zip the back of the dress.

She smiled at him in the mirror. "Almost cheating but thank you."

"You're welcome." He looked at her in the mirror. "The color is too severe for you."

Delaney rolled her eyes. "Yeah…"

The next dress was a deep, almost black, purple that shimmered slightly as she moved. As he stood behind her looking at her in the mirror, his expression showed her how much that particular dress worked. "This one is a keeper."

"It sure is." He kissed the back of her neck. "And I get to take you out wearing it."

Delaney tried on two other dresses, one she didn't like, one James didn't like. Finally slipping back into her clothes, she smiled. "Okay. Done. Let me go pay, and you can text Thomas to find out where we're meeting them."

"I'll pay for the dress."

Delaney raised an eyebrow at him. "No, you won't. Thank you, but no." She touched his face, not wanting to hurt his feelings. "I don't need you to buy me clothes. But you can buy me dinner."

"I can do that."

After she paid, they started to leave the store, until James saw the lingerie department. Seeing his grin, she smiled. "Want to shop some more?"

"Absolutely."

Walking through the racks of lacy garments, Delaney could feel how badly she was blushing. Suddenly James stopped by a rack. His voice was serious. "These."

On the rack were various colors of tiny lacy bras, panties, and thongs. Reaching out to touch them, even Delaney had to admit it was like touching the softest of silk. "I can do these."

"This I'm buying you." It was a declaration, not an offer or a question.

Looking at him, Delaney saw the raw desire in his eyes. "That works." She smiled. "You're buying, you pick the colors and styles."

Minutes later, the clerk handed James the beautiful bag with the undergarments inside wrapped in tissue paper.

They strolled out of the store, holding hands, James carrying the shopping bags. Seeing them, Pam raised an eyebrow. "You forgave him too damn easily."

James tried not to laugh. "Thanks, Pam."

Delaney looked up at James, then smiled at her best friend. "He groveled pretty well."

Pam shook her head. "Fine." She grinned outright at James. "Do it again, and I'll kick you in the balls."

"Don't I know it."

Chapter Twenty-eight

Back at her house, James carried the bags inside. "Where do you want them?"

"On the guest room bed."

After putting them down, James came back into the kitchen where Delaney was standing with a glass of water. Taking the glass and putting it down, he took both of her hands in his. "Laney. Thank you for a great day. Thank you for forgiving me." He stepped closer and put a gentle finger under her chin to have her look up at him. "Thank you for loving me and letting me love you."

"Likewise." She stretched up, kissed him hard, and took his hand. "And now I want to go to bed with you." She stopped suddenly, so unexpectedly that he almost ran into her. "You are staying, aren't you?"

With a laugh, he scooped her up and put her over his shoulder. "Yup! I'm staying. You didn't ask me to, but I'm staying anyway."

Delaney giggled happily. "And what if I told you to go home?"

Placing her on the bed, he leaned down over her. "I'd beg you to let me stay."

"I thought you'd never beg."

"No, I said I wouldn't blush." He reached down to start unbuttoning her blouse. "Beg? That I'd do."

Reaching out to tug him closer so she could start unbuttoning his shirt, she said, "Just make love to me."

"My pleasure."

She giggled. "And mine."

As he sat down on the side of the bed to take off his shoes, he commented, "Laney?"

"Yes?"

To be clear, never, ever have I bought lingerie for any woman before today." Standing, he unbuckled his belt, and removed his pants. "I want you to know that."

Delaney looked up at him, seeing how serious his face was. "Thank you."

Completely naked now, he looked at her. "Why do you still have clothes on?"

Naked in seconds, Delaney chuckled. "Better?"

Lying down next to her, James smiled. "So, want to play a game?"

She knew what he was suggesting, but quipped, "Crazy eights?"

"Not quite."

"Then what?"

"I want to suggest something. If you want to do it, great, if not, fine."

"Okay."

"I want you to get a scarf, and I want to tie the scarf to your headboard. Then I want you to hold onto that scarf, lying on your back, and you can't let go."

"Okay."

"Then, when you're in that position, I'm going to touch you as I want. And you can't move or let go of that scarf."

She could feel heat surging through her. Damn! He was turning her on with his words. "Okay."

"And if you let go, or if you move around, I'm going to make you turn over, and I'm going to spank you one time for not following my directions. If you don't move or let go, no spanking."

"Okay." She could feel her body already pulsing with need just from his directions!

"Then, when you come, I'm going to turn you over, kneeling away from me—still holding onto that scarf—and I'm going to slide inside you, hard and fast."

"Okay."

"And at any time, if you want to stop, or you don't like what we're doing, tell me, and I'll stop, I promise."

"Okay."

"Okay?" He smiled at her, trying to gauge her brain's reaction to his words. He already knew what her body wanted, the proof in how tight and proud her nipples were at his words.

She smiled, sitting up. "More than okay. Let me get a scarf." She slid off the bed, and soundlessly walked across the carpeted floor to her closet, returning in seconds with a silk scarf. Holding it out to him she said, "You were the Boy Scout, you tie it."

As Delaney laid back down on the cool sheets, James tied the scarf to the bedpost. He leaned down to kiss her lips gently. "Love you."

"Love you." She grinned devilishly. "Let's play."

"Stretch your arms up over your head and take the scarf in your hands." She did as he requested. "Now don't let go." Suddenly Delaney realized—feeling foolish that she hadn't understood it before—that he was giving her the sense of being tied up, without actually doing it, giving her time to see if she liked it or not. Just feeling the heat rising in her body, she knew already that she liked this game.

Then he started a slow and equally sensual and tortuous exploration of her body—touching, licking, and stroking her. Delaney could feel how wet she was becoming as he continued his journey. Feeling emboldened and curious, Delaney decided that she wanted to see what would happen, and how it would feel, if she broke the rules. Knowing exactly what she was doing, she let go of the scarf with her right hand, and put it down on his head, weaving her fingers through his dark hair, urging his head down toward the apex of her thighs.

With her touch, James stilled. Lifting his head, he saw her gazing at him, clearly knowing what she was doing. He tried not to smile. "You just broke the rules, Laney. You know what that means, don't you?"

"I do."

"Turn over."

Delaney turned over and felt James trail his fingers down her backbone, then his hand moved, and she felt a sharp smack on her bottom. Rather than painful, Delaney realized in amazement that the little shock caused a huge tidal wave of desire to flood through her.

James leaned down to kiss the same spot. "That's what happens when you don't follow the rules." He stroked her backside. "Turn over."

Delaney turned, and he could see from the look in her eyes that she was as aroused as he was. "Hold the scarf again."

She did as he ordered, and James continued to explore her now flushed skin, his fingers coming closer to the V between her legs. Lightly stroking her curls, he smiled seeing her struggle not move with his touch. "Good girl. Now spread your legs for me."

She did, and he moved so that he could look lovingly at her, breathing in her scent before he ran a light finger down between her legs. "You are so very wet, my love. I think you like our game."

"I do!"

"I thought you might." He took his other hand and gently spread her lips. "You smell so good, and are so wet, I can't believe it." He touched his fingertip to her nub and watched her muscles clench as she tried not to rear up to meet his touch. "Now I'm going to lick you slowly, put my tongue in you, and suck you until you come. And you can't move."

Her voice was strained to her own ears. "I won't move."

Then he did as he said he was going to, and Delaney thought she would lose her mind with the sensations he was causing. Being unable to touch him or hold his head in place, to just let him do as he wanted, was so sexy. She'd never felt anything like it before. He was in control of when she would find the release she craved so much, and it was incredible.

As Delaney got closer, she tried to keep still. He stopped, and she whimpered. "Delaney, what am I going to do when you come?"

She tried to slow her breathing. "You're going to tell me to turn over, and then…"

"And then?"

She looked at him, straight in the eyes, and said, "You're going to fuck me hard and fast, until we both come again."

And it wasn't long before that was just what he did. Delaney almost screamed as the first orgasm hit her, leaving her shaking with its power. As she was still reeling, James gently but firmly turned her over, and within seconds, she felt his hands firmly on her hips. "Now, I'm going to fuck you, love of mine."

The sensation of his hips slamming into her over and over was so intense that even as she could still feel the aftershocks of the first orgasm, Delany could already feel her body start to coil again. She craved him going deeper and harder, loving the intensity of the sensations. Within minutes, Delaney could feel her body beginning to clench, and heard James say, "God, Laney, you feel so good, you're getting ready again, and it's like your body is grabbing mine."

His words pushed her over the edge and—with a shout—Delaney was racked by the strongest orgasm of her life, making her see stars for a moment. As she struggled to make sense of everything she was feeling, she felt James surge forward, pouring into her with a groan. Then she felt him slide forward, gently lying them both down on the bed—still buried deep inside her. Even in her afterglow, Delaney realized he was bracing himself so that his entire weight wasn't on top of her.

Long moments later, he rolled to the side, reaching up to pull the scarf from where Delaney still clutched it. He kissed her shoulder. "You can let go now."

Her eyes were closed, but she smiled. "But what if I don't want the game to be over?"

He stroked her arm. "I promise we can play again, whenever you want."

Rolling onto her side, she opened her eyes to look at him. "Jesus, James. Have we had enough new experiences for one day?"

"I think so." He took her into his arms, pulling the duvet up over them. "Good night, love."

"Good night."

Chapter Twenty-nine

Two weeks later, James pulled into the parking lot at Green Airport. "So, I'll come get you when you come home, and your car will be at my house."

"Exactly." She was digging around in her purse, checking to see that her tickets were still where she'd put them. "Thanks for driving me."

"My pleasure." He looked her over while her focus was occupied with her purse. "I still would rather be going with you, but at least I get you for the night when you return."

Delaney stopped and looked up at him. "You know I'd love to have you go with me, but between presenting tomorrow, and co-facilitating discussion groups, I'm going to be out straight for the next two days." Her grin was sexy. "Too busy to even enjoy having you in my hotel room. This way, you have two full days and nights to paint around the clock if you want, then come get me Saturday afternoon, and take me to your place for the rest of the weekend." She reached out to take his hand. "I even told Luther I wouldn't be home until after work on Monday, so I can stay Sunday night too."

That was better than he'd expected. "Great."

In the airport, Delaney quickly checked in and walked toward the safety gates. She let James carry her bag. As they got close to the checkpoint, she stopped. "Okay, time for me to go through the screening."

He put her bag down and opened his arms. Delaney came forward, wrapping her arms around him before tipping her head up for a kiss. Long moments later, he pulled back, stroking her curls away from her face. "Have fun, be careful, call me when you can, and know that I love you."

"I will—all of those things—and I love you too."

With that, Delaney picked up her carryon and turned toward the gate, giving him a saucy look back over her shoulder. James stood watching her until she'd passed through security, about to turn away when he saw her sit down in the secure lounge and put her feet up on her bag. In that moment, James' mind flashed back to that day in the Chicago airport. In amazement, he looked at Delaney, suddenly seeing the black leggings, gray tunic, black shoes, black bag, and the white blonde curls as if for the first time. Did she know?

James turned away, thinking about what this meant. Of course she knew. She'd seen and heard the conversation. Why hadn't she said something?

Delaney was thankful when she stepped into her hotel room in Savannah. After a quick trip to the bathroom, she walked back into the bedroom area, and opened the manila envelope that the desk clerk had handed her.

Pulling the piece of paper from the envelope, Delaney's eyes widened in shock. It was a color copy of a sketch that James had made, clearly of that day in Chicago. The drawing showed her sitting in the lounge, her feet up on her bag, her rainbow scarf knitting cascading down from her hands. It was a stunningly beautiful picture, even as much as she was still uncomfortable of him drawing her.

Delaney sat down on the bed. How did he know? She hadn't told him. Luther wouldn't have told him. How did he figure it out, and was he mad that she hadn't said anything?

Old habits die hard. Delaney could feel her stomach clench. What if he was angry? How would he react? For a moment, she could feel fear start to race through her body. Anger meant pain, always had.

Wait a minute! her rational mind screamed. If he was mad, he wouldn't have sent her the drawing. The drawing was his way of telling her he knew, and that he loved her. Right?

Delaney stood up and walked to the window, looking down and across the river to the busy scene of River Street. The only way to know how he felt was to either call or text him. Texting would be safer, but she wasn't going to really know how he felt until she heard his voice. Time to call him!

Just then her phone buzzed with a text. Striding over to the bed, Delaney picked up the phone and read James' text. *The airline says you landed about 90 minutes ago, you all checked in?*

Delaney stood there, looking at the text, and a slow smile spread across her face. Clearly, he was second-guessing his decision to send the drawing as much as she was worrying about his reaction to her not telling him. She hit speed dial and started to laugh when he answered on the first ring. "What took you so long? It almost rang one full time."

"Funny. You're funny."

"I know I am!"

"How was your flight?"

"Crowded, bumpy, and the guy next to me smelled funny. It was a normal flight."

"And you're at the hotel?"

"I am." She paused. "And I got the most amazing gift when I arrived."

Standing in his kitchen, James let out a deep breath, relieved at hearing the tone of her voice. "Really? What'd you get?"

"This absolutely fabulous drawing. Somebody must have been stalking me when I was in the airport in Chicago almost two years ago."

"Do you like it?"

The man was a world-renowned artist, and yet Delaney could hear the insecurity in his voice. "I love it, James!"

"Good."

"When did you do it?"

"That night, sitting on the plane. You were such a striking visual, I couldn't get you out of my mind." He chuckled. "I still can't. But then it wasn't a sexual thing, or a love thing, it was the combination of colors and lines that caught my eye."

"Are you mad?"

"About what, Laney?"

"That I didn't tell you?"

He paused, shocked by her question. "No! Of course not, baby. What you did that night was amazing, and it meant so much. I tried to get your name that night to thank you, and they wouldn't give it to me. Thank you, period."

Delaney flopped back on the bed, relief flowing through her. "So, I need to tell you something."

"Of course."

"I could hear you talking to the airline attendant. I had made the decision to offer you my seat just from hearing the conversation, but after I saw your face, I..." Delaney could feel how red she was becoming.

"You...?"

"I thought about you after that. I didn't know who you were, but I admit that…"

"What?"

"Sometimes I dreamed of you. I knew I'd never see you again, so maybe it was safe for me to dream that way. Then we met, and all I could think of was that you were standing in front of me, and I didn't know what to do. I knew you wouldn't know who I was, but it was still intense."

At her words, James could feel a rush of arousal. His voice deepened. "So, you're in a hotel room in Savannah fucking Georgia, I'm in Rhode Island, and you drop on me that you dreamt of me after that night?"

Delaney felt a rush of heat race through her. "Yes, that's what I'm telling you."

"Dreams like we met, took a walk, ate pizza?"

Delaney knew when she was being baited. "No. Not pizza dreams. Hand holding, kissing dreams. A few naked dreams."

"That's it! Get back to that damn airport and come home! You tell me that and you aren't here? Jesus, do you have any idea what you are doing to me?"

"I do! The same thing you're doing to me." Delaney stretched. "And since I'm not brave enough yet for phone sex, how about you tell me about your day?"

For the next ten minutes, they chatted, then Delaney stood up. "Babe, I'm starving. I'm going to go get some food."

"Sounds good."

"Can I call you later?"

"Of course!"

Two days later, Delaney walked down the concourse and saw James waiting for her. Her heart jumped. Would she ever not feel such a thrill seeing him?

Reaching him, she wasn't surprised when he picked her up in a tight hug, kissing her hungrily. Setting her carefully back down on her feet, he picked up her bag. "Ready to go home?"

"I am."

They spoke very little until they were in the car. As he put the car in gear, Delaney looked at him and grinned. "So, while my phone was off, I got a text from your mom inviting us to dinner tonight, then got your response saying no." Innocently, she asked, "You don't want to have dinner with your parents?"

Stopping at the kiosk to pay for parking, James turned and looked at her, his eyes gazing at her ravenously. "No, love my parents, love to get together with them. That's why I said I thought brunch or lunch tomorrow might work. But tonight? Tonight, I'm taking you home, making love to you first, then we'll eat dinner, and I don't want to be around anyone other than you."

"And if I wanted to have dinner with them tonight?" Delaney tried to keep a straight face.

"Then, after I have reminded you that you are mine—heart, soul and body—we can drive over to my parents, but it may take a while."

"Hmmm."

"And what does 'hmmm' mean?"

"It means I like your plan."

Late the next morning, James put on his sunglasses. "Ready?"

Delaney looked over at him. "I'm ready."

At his parents' house, James parked near the front door. As they walked in, he shouted, "Mom, we're here!"

Gail popped her head out of the kitchen to see them. "Good! Come on in here and keep me company."

A stew bubbled on the stove, and the table was set for four, with a huge green salad in the middle, a loaf of crusty bread and an open bottle of wine. After hugging Gail, Delaney looked around. "Anything I can do to help?"

"No, sweetheart! Take a seat, pour yourself some wine and tell me about the conference. We're about ten minutes from food being ready."

James watched in amusement as Delaney told his mother all about the conference, much more than she'd told him. Of course, this was Gail's area of expertise too.

When the stew was ready, Gail pulled out bowls, and smiled. "Okay, gang. Time to eat. Someone get Bob, please."

Delaney jumped up. "I will. Where is he?"

Gail smiled. "Last door on the right. He's in his study. When he tells you just a few more minutes, tell him I said to move it."

Delaney walked down the hall, barely glancing at the family photos that lined the walls. What would it be like to have a family? What would it be like to have a past that you were proud to talk about?

At the open door, Delaney knocked and poked her head in. "Robert? Gail says lunch is …" Her voice trailed off as she saw what he was doing and was immediately transported back in time.

Robert sat on a stool at a long worktable, a bright light illuminating the magnifying glass through which he was looking at something held in vice grips. How many times had she seen her own father sitting just that way? The sudden wave of emotion hit her. She *did* have a good memory of him!

Robert looked up, seeing Delaney standing there, her face pure white. "Delaney! So good to see you, sweetie. Come in!"

Delaney walked into the room in a fog. The older man stood and came over to hug her. "Come in, let me show you my hobby."

Her voice showed a sense of wonder. "You tie flies."

Robert was surprised. "I do. You know fly tying?"

She looked down at her feet, suddenly shy. "I do. My…" She swallowed, and her voice almost came out as a whisper. "My dad loved to fly fish, and he taught me how to tie flies and to fish."

Robert realized that both his son and his wife had clearly told him that Delaney never spoke of her past, so he wasn't going to ask questions. "Then come over and see what I'm tying and give me your opinion."

In the kitchen, Gail and James chatted and sipped their wine, not realizing how much time had passed. Suddenly, Gail looked at the wall clock. "Where the hell are they? Delaney went to get him almost twenty minutes ago."

James stood up, stretching. "Dad's probably boring her to death, telling her about the friggin' flies, and she's too sweet to walk away. I'll go get them."

"I'll go with you."

They went down the hall, talking quietly, but as they got close to the study, they could hear the laughter from inside, and they both looked at each other quizzically. Pushing the door open, James was shocked to see Delaney perched on a stool next to his father, tying a fly and grinning broadly. Just as they walked in, Robert exclaimed enthusiastically, "That's it, my girl! You've still got it!"

Delaney reached out and hugged him, and as she did, James saw the sheen of tears in her eyes. "Thank you! That was so much fun."

Standing up, with his arm still around her shoulders, he asked, "Want to go try them out some weekend soon?"

Before James could jump in and make an excuse for why Delaney wouldn't want to go stand in a stream all day just like his sons, he watched in amazement as she looked up at Robert with absolute joy, and said, "I'd love to!"

The sun was setting over the ocean as they drove back toward James' house. He looked at Delaney, seeing her seemingly lost in her thoughts. "You really want to go fly fishing with my dad? You weren't just being polite?"

Delaney took a moment to figure out how to respond. "No, I wasn't being polite at all. I'd love to go with him. I fly fished when I was little, until I was eight, and I loved it."

For a split second, James wondered anew what was in her past that kept her from talking about it, and he felt questions welling up in him. He tried to keep his voice neutral. "Who'd you fish with?"

"My dad."

That was it. She didn't say another word about it, and James could feel that she was getting anxious just saying that much. He reached out and squeezed her hand. "Well, all I know is that my dad is so excited about going fishing with you, he can't stand it. He dragged us all up there at times, and none of us liked it, so having someone who doesn't automatically glaze over when he starts talking about the most recent fly he's made is a gift for him." His voice softened. "Thank you."

Delaney turned and looked at him. "My pleasure."

At his house, James asked her, "What do you want to do?"

"I want to go for a walk."

"Okay."

A few minutes later, they walked down his driveway, hand in hand, and slowly strolled through the neighborhood, staying close to the waterfront, not talking. James sensed her mind was wrestling with something, so he just kept quiet.

They had walked for almost a half hour, now walking under the streetlights, when Delaney said quietly, "My dad and I didn't have a good relationship. Fly fishing was the only thing that we did together that was consistently positive."

"Oh." What else could he say? He could hear the repressed pain in her voice.

"And seeing your dad tying the fly today, it reminded me of the fishing times, and it gave me a moment of a good memory."

"That's why you looked like you were ready to cry when we came in."

"Yes." She squeezed his hand. "Please don't ask about it. I know you want to, and I know that it's unfair that I won't let you ask, but I'm not ready yet."

"I won't." He stopped and reached out to pull her into his arms, hugging her tightly, as he whispered in her ear, "I love you, and I can wait until you're ready."

"Thank you."

Monday night, Delaney crawled into bed feeling tired and out-of-sorts. The workday had gone well, as had her board meeting. In her heart, she knew that her restless state had way more to do with revisiting fly tying than anything else. For so many years—almost twenty of them—she had not allowed herself the luxury of thinking back to her father. Why had she irritated him so much? Why?

Huddling under the covers, she tried all her most effective mindfulness techniques until she felt her body began to relax.

Hours later she awoke with a start, her dreams of tying flies ending with a sharp crack across her face.

Tomorrow and Yesterday

Chapter Thirty

Two weeks later, coming back from his whirlwind trip to San Francisco, James was disappointed when Delaney was too swamped at work to see him that night. When they texted the next morning, he was surprised when she said she probably wouldn't be able to get together that night either. James tried to keep the frustration out of his messages, feeling slightly better when her last message said, *I miss you like crazy. Can't wait to see you, but today/tonight are too busy. Love you.*

So, late that afternoon, he was shocked when his cell rang, and he saw that it was the main office at the Center. "Hello?"

"James? It's Alyssa."

"Is Delaney okay?" Fear hit him.

"Yes." She paused. "No. That's why I'm calling. Laney would be rip-shit if she knew."

James sat down on a stool. "What's going on?"

"Delaney is sick as a dog. She's been since the day you left on your trip. It started like a cold but now—"

James interrupted, "Yeah, she was coughing that night when I talked to her."

"Have you talked to her today?"

"No…"

"Did you try to call her?"

"I did."

"She didn't answer, right? And she texted you back?"

"Yeah."

"If you heard how lousy she sounds, you'd be here, dragging her off to the doctor. The nurse suspects either bronchitis or pneumonia. She won't go home, and she won't go to see the doctor." Alyssa sounded exasperated. "I mean she *never* takes time off for being sick, but this is really bad."

James stood up, moving toward the front hall. "Do you have the name of her doctor?"

"I do."

"Can you text it to me?"

"I can."

"I'll be there in a half-hour. I'll get Luther to pick up her car, and I'll take her home."

"She's going to be mad as hell."

He laughed. "I like when she gets mad."

James and Luther walked into the Center, and as they started down the main hallway, they could hear someone coughing like crazy. Luther shrugged at James. "I haven't seen her in days, and she's kept the TV or music going…"

At Alyssa's desk, James said, "Luther, stay here."

"You got it."

James knocked on the closed door and heard a raspy voice call. "Come in."

He stepped inside and took in the sight of Delaney in concern. Her flushed cheeks spoke of a fever. He could see she was shivering, and as she looked at him, she whispered, "Shit," and started to cough, needing to steady herself on her desk.

He tried to smile. "Not your usual greeting, I guess you didn't expect me."

"What are you doing here?"

"Your staff is worried about you. I'm here to take you to the doctor, then take you home. Your choice, my house or yours."

Her voice rose. "I'm not leaving."

"You are." He moved closer to touch her cheek, finding it burning with fever. "You most certainly are leaving. The choice you have is to do so relatively willingly, or if need be, I'll haul you kicking and screaming out of here. I brought Luther with me so if you call the police, he can get rid of them."

"Not funny!"

"I'm not being funny." He took her hands, rubbing her icy fingers between his own. "You're sick. You need to get seen, and I'm taking you there now."

"You can't take me to the doctor! I don't have an appointment."

"Yes, you do." He looked at his watch. "In a half-hour."

"How the fuck do I have an appointment?"

"I made one for you. I got the doctor's information from Alyssa. Don't be mad at her. I called and you have an appointment." His voice was matter of fact. "We're going now."

"I'm not going. You can't do this!"

"I can, I did, and I will." He stroked her face. "I love you, and for whatever reason, you're not willing to take care of yourself right now, so I'm taking that out of your hands." His voice softened. "Come on, Laney, don't fight me on this. Go to the doctor, and if she says you're fine to go back to work tomorrow, I won't interfere. Just make us all feel better by getting checked. Please."

Delaney stood there glaring at him. "Fine!"

In the parking lot, Luther took her keys, kissing her on the top of her head. "Love you, Lulu. Let me know what the doctor says."

James was surprised when the nurse came to the waiting room door. "Mr. McDaniels, can you come back, please?"

James followed the nurse down the hall, not sure why he'd been called in to the appointment. As he stepped into the examining room, he stifled a smile as he saw how angry Delaney was.

The doctor looked at James and rolled her eyes. "James, nice to meet you. Little Ms. Sunshine here has signed a release for me to talk to you today."

Delaney started to cough. "Fuck you, Cheyanne."

Seeing his shocked expression, the doctor laughed. "We went to college together."

"Oh."

"Anyway. Delaney is unhappy with me right now. She has pneumonia. Double pneumonia. She has a hell of a fever, and needs rest, fluids, and no stress. She's not contagious, but she can't work until at least next Monday. I want to see her first thing on Monday, and if her lungs are clearer and she hasn't had a fever in over twenty-four hours, I'll allow her to return to work." Her voice grew more serious. "Laney, seriously, another 12 to 24 hours, and you would have been in the hospital. Someone our age shouldn't get sick like this. You need to take this as a warning and be more careful about your health."

Turning back to James, the doctor continued, "I've called in an inhaler, an antibiotic, cough syrup, and an expectorant. They'll be ready at the Walgreens around the corner in about ten minutes. Then, she needs to go home, go to bed, and stay there for the next couple days. Can you make sure she does that?"

"Absolutely."

James got back in the car with a white paper bag full of medications. Delaney was leaning back in the passenger seat, her eyes closed. Putting on his seatbelt, he said, "I got everything. Do you want to go home or to my house?"

Even to her own ears, Delaney knew she sounded hostile, but couldn't seem to help it. "Do I really have a choice?"

"Delaney! I'm offering you a choice right now. Your house or mine. I can stay at yours, in which case I'll take you home, make sure Luther can keep you company for a while, then run home to get some clothes. Or we can stop at your place, get anything you need, and go to my house. Which do you prefer?"

He was being reasonable. Deep down, she knew it. "Neither. I want to go home, and I can take care of myself."

"Not happening. You can barely walk right now, let alone take care of yourself. What do you want to do?"

"Your house, okay, your house! Just go there. I have leggings there, it'll be fine."

Where had his sweet, agreeable Delaney gone? James was facing a snarling, hostile feverish shadow of the woman he loved. "Okay. That's our plan."

At his house, Delaney wanted to storm out of the car and into the house, but as she stood up, she swayed with dizziness. James saw her, rushed over, and wrapped his arm around her. "You can be pissed off at me after you get in bed."

"Fine."

In the bedroom, Delaney stood staring ahead, dazed. James walked into the closet and found her leggings. "What do you want for a shirt?"

"Could I borrow a sweatshirt?"

"Of course."

Minutes later, Delaney came out of the bathroom, dressed in her leggings and his Yale Law hoodie, which hung to her knees. Tiredly, she walked over to the bed, seeing he'd already turned back the covers. His voice was gentle. "Once you're settled, I'll get you something to drink and your medicine."

Delaney looked at him, and her eyes filled with tears. James jumped forward, wrapping her shaking body in his arms. "Laney, what is it, sweetie?"

Her voice was muffled in his shirt. "I'm being such a bitch to you, and you're just trying to be nice to me."

He smiled. "You aren't being a bitch."

She pulled back, steadying herself with one hand on his chest. "You said you'd never lie to me."

"What?"

"I *am* being a bitch. I know that. I'm trying to apologize."

He pulled her close, rubbing her back. "Okay, yes, you were a bit difficult. It's okay. You're here, you're about to do what the doctor ordered, and I can make sure you are okay."

"Okay." She brushed away the tears in irritation. "I haven't stayed home sick since I was eight years old."

"Are you serious?"

She nodded, looking at her feet. "If I don't do my part, others suffer. That's why I make myself go."

"Laney, listen to me: I get toughing it out, but you were ready to drop. You could have caused yourself real physical harm." He motioned toward the bed. "Time to get in bed, time to rest, time to let go of your ideas of what you need to do for others."

She climbed slowly under the blankets, realizing how much every inch of her body ached. Smoothing the covers over her, he kissed her forehead. "You're the kindest, sweetest, most loving person I know. You take care of everyone else, and sometimes you forget about yourself." He ran his index finger down her nose. "So, my princess, now you're stuck with me watching you like a hawk until Monday."

Delaney looked up at him, her eyes and tone serious. "Okay."

"Okay?"

She nodded. "Okay. I admit defeat."

He smiled. "Finally! I'm going to get your medicine, then you take a nap for a bit. Later, we'll have dinner, and I can get you settled on the couch if you want to get out of bed for a bit."

Her voice was unsure. "Will you still sleep with me tonight?"

"Try to keep me away!"

Luther hung up the phone after talking with James. Feeling slightly more optimistic after hearing the diagnosis, Luther took a steadying breath, then walked into his office. Kneeling, he carefully punched in the security code to his safe, then pulled a battered file from inside.

Sitting at his desk, he scanned the familiar pages until he found what he was looking for. No wonder Lulu wouldn't take a sick day. How he wished he could share the reason with James.

Shaking his head with grief and sadness, Luther put the file back and locked the safe. Taking the note he'd written while on the phone with James, he let himself into Delaney's house, moving through the rooms until he stood in front of her bureau. Carefully, he found the requested items, piling them carefully on her bed so he could deliver them in the morning. Just as he was about to close her sock drawer, he noticed something. Slightly ashamed of what he was doing, Luther pulled the battered frame out from under her wool socks and found himself staring at a picture of a young Delaney sitting on a dock with a curly haired little boy. He looked so much like her, it had to be her brother. With shaking hands, he tucked it back under the socks. "My poor Lulu."

Chapter Thirty-one

As the weeks went by, James and Delaney had settled into a routine. Most Friday and Saturday nights, they stayed at his house. Mondays—when she didn't have a board meeting—and Tuesdays, he stayed at her place. Wednesdays, he joined Luther and Delaney for dinner, but didn't usually spend the night. With each passing week, it became more and more like they were living together, but James realized his frustration was growing in that he wanted them to live together all the time. Each night they were apart, he spent far too much time stewing over how to change the situation until one day his frustration boiled over.

His voice showed his shock and irritation as he said, "You seriously won't go? All I'm asking is that you take Friday and go to New York with me. Please."

She shook her head, still peeling a carrot at her kitchen sink, not looking at him. "I can't. I can't take the day, I have too many meetings, and I really can't take another weekend where I don't get any work done. I did nothing for work last weekend."

"Which was my fault?"

She dropped the carrot to turn to look at him. "It's not a fault thing. It's reality. I need to get the quarterly reports done, and so I need to work this weekend."

"Then come up Friday after work, you can work when you need to, and we'll still be together."

"You know you don't really mean that. If I pull out my laptop there, you're going to feel ignored, and then both of us will be miserable." She walked over to tug on his shirt, pulling him close so she could kiss him briefly. "Go to New York, do what you need to do, and next time, with more notice, I can go with you."

"I don't want to go without you. That means we won't see each other for an entire weekend!"

"I know. But I can't go this time."

"You couldn't go last time either!"

Her voice held a warning. "James, don't do this. I love you; you love me. We have different work lives. I'm not able to go this weekend, and I'll miss you, but I understand that you have to go. I'm not pissed at you for needing to go, so why are you mad at me for staying?"

She had a point. Sighing, he moved forward to pull her into his arms. "Fine." He kissed her hungrily. "Then forget about dinner and come to bed with me. We can order take out later."

"Now you're thinking clearly."

The Monday after he returned, he stood in complete disbelief, looking out at the waves as he talked to Laney on the phone. "You're kidding me, Laney. I haven't seen you since Wednesday. You wouldn't go with me, now you're too busy to get together tonight?"

"I have a board meeting! You know that, James. It's on our shared calendar, for God's sake. This isn't a surprise."

He sighed. "I know." He rubbed his forehead. "I'm sorry. I just miss you."

"I miss you too." A noise in the background could be heard. "I need to go, but I'll call you when I get home tonight, I promise."

"Sounds good. I love you."

"Love you, too."

Tuesday's plans got scrapped because James needed to meet with his agent, and Wednesday Luther needed a ride to a medical appointment, so by Thursday when Delaney worked at Mercy, James felt like he was losing his mind. Getting in his car midday Friday with a grilled chicken salad for Laney and a sandwich for himself, he drove to the center on autopilot.

After visiting with Alyssa for a moment and giving her the iced coffee, he knew she loved, he walked down the hall to Laney's office unannounced. She was on the phone as he came in, and for a moment he gratefully drank in the sight of her but realized how very tired and pale she looked.

Standing in the door to her office, he waited until she was done with the call, then said quietly, "Hi."

The immediate look of joy on her face banished his deep worries that she'd been avoiding him. "What are you doing here?"

"I decided that if I can't see you at night, then I could at least drop by to see your face for a minute, so I remember what you look like." He held up the bag. "And I figured you might need lunch."

She walked toward him, holding out her hand to pull him further into the office. Then she pushed the door shut with her toe, and wrapped her arms around him tightly, kissing him.

Desire slammed into him like a tidal wave—as did relief— since she clearly missed him as much as he'd missed her. Realizing they were in her office, and they could be interrupted at any minute, he reluctantly pulled back to look at her. "Come and sit down, let me see you eat something, and then I promise I'll get out of your hair."

He watched happily as she dug into her salad, giving their conversation her full attention. Once they were done eating, she picked up the wrappers and trash, and threw them away. Walking back to the table, she sat down facing him, and took his hands. "I owe you an apology."

"For what?" He was confused.

"For not making you a priority this week." She looked down at their hands. "I love you, but I don't think I made you feel that way this week, and I'm sorry for that. You're the most important part of my life, and I kept blowing you off."

Her words hit him, and he smiled. "You don't owe me an apology, Laney. Yes, I did feel ignored, but I also get that you have more rigidity in your schedule than in mine."

"Thank you."

He looked at her intently. "Laney, will you move in with me? Or me with you?"

Her eyes widened. "What?"

"Let's live together." His voice became stronger. "Let's make it official. One house. I don't care which, just let's live together."

"You mean it?"

"I do."

She sat and looked at him seriously, and for a moment, his heart sank. Then a little smile started at the corner of her mouth. "You pop in for lunch and ask me to move in with you? I would've thought that you'd have at least brought flowers for that one?"

He started to chuckle. "You once told me that you didn't need flowers and candles, remember? You want flowers? Say yes and I'll bring you more flowers than you can imagine."

She leaned back in her chair. "You understand how crazy my schedule is? You're okay with that?"

"I'm more than okay with that. I would rather have you come home in the middle of the night and get in bed with me, than wait up until you text me to say you're home, then miss you for the rest of the night." He reached out to stroke her face. "My life is with you, whether at your place or mine. I know there are times when one of us will be away, or working late, or need to work at home until all hours. I get that. I just want to wake up in the morning next to you, have coffee with you, hear you swear at your mascara every morning. I don't want to feel like we are commuting in this relationship."

She stood up and walked over to him, smiling as he put his hands on her hips. She leaned down and whispered, "Yes. I'll live with you."

He jumped to his feet, picking her up in his arms and kissing her fiercely, which she returned with equal fervor.

Pulling back reluctantly, she kissed him again briefly. "We can talk details later. Right now, I have recess duty."

"You're coming over tonight?"

"Of course I am."

"Dinner out or in?"

Her smile was slow and sexy. "In. I want dinner in. Just us, no company. No phones, no email, just us."

"Sounds like a plan."

Tomorrow and Yesterday

Chapter Thirty-two

After work, Delaney drove home deep in thought. Pulling into her parking spot, she got out of the car slowly. How was she going to tell Luther? Should she ask James to move in with her here?

Opening the door to her house, she felt the familiar rush of pleasure at being in her space, but she had to admit that she felt that same rush at James'—even more so because of his presence there. Grabbing a glass of water, she opened the deck door and strode out onto it. "Luther?"

He was in his living room, and she could hear the Red Sox game in the background. "In here."

"Can I come over?"

"Since when do you ask?"

Hopping the railing, she walked into his living room, plopping on the couch next to his chair. She watched the game in silence for a few minutes.

Luther muted the game. "What's on your mind, Lulu?"

She leaned back against the couch, her stomach in knots. How was she going to say it? No matter what, his life was going to change too, and they'd been a pair for a long, long time. "I have news."

"You're finally moving in with him?"

Anger filled her. "How the hell do you do that? You make me crazy, old man. Just once I'd like to tell you something without you knowing it first!"

He grinned. "So I'm right?"

Delaney swallowed. "Yeah, you're right."

"And you were afraid to tell me?"

"Not afraid, that's not the right emotion, more…"

He stood up and came over to the couch, sitting down beside her. Taking her hand in his, he looked at her intently. "Delaney, my girl, you listen to me. You're the daughter we weren't able to have. Every day, Sheila and I gave thanks that you moved in next to us, and when she was dying, she was so thankful that you'd be around to keep me company after she was gone. I love having you as my neighbor, and I love you, period. But I also want you to be happy, and to have your own life. You're meant to be with James. You are. I really like that boy too, and I have no worries that you'll still be my Lulu, even if you are living with him, even if you marry him. You're stuck with me."

Delaney started to cry, feeling relief fill her. Luther pulled her close, letting her cry on his shoulder. His voice softened. "Lulu, you're meant to be happy. Be happy with James. And you still get me."

She hugged him. "Thank you. I really love you, Luther."

"Where will you live?"

"We haven't decided. I'm going there tonight, and I said we'd talk details this weekend."

"Do you want my opinion?"

"Of course I do."

"Live there, chickadee. That place is meant for a couple, for a family. You can make an office space for you there, and he has his studio. To make your place work for you as a couple and for his work would be difficult. It would save a lot of time, stress, and money to live at his place, and you both love his house."

After leaving Luther's house, Delaney got in the car. The old man had followed her to the vehicle and was leaning into the open window looking at her. Her voice was squeaky with emotion. "You aren't getting rid of me. And you're still going to have dinner with me on Wednesdays."

"Go home, sweetie."

At James', Delaney pulled in slowly, looking at the house and the ocean beyond. No matter how much she wanted to fight it—because she was afraid to leave Luther on his own—this was where she wanted to live. It truly was. And it had been since the first time she'd driven into the driveway.

She was surprised that James wasn't waiting for her at the door as he normally was. She'd texted him when she'd left her house.

Just then, she realized there was something on the door, and recognized it as a long-stemmed red rose. With a giggle, she strode up the walk, carefully removed the rose and opened the door, knowing it would be unlocked.

Flowers were everywhere. Bouquets, single flowers, all around the foyer, and lining the hall to the kitchen. Delaney looked up, seeing James leaning against the arched frame leading to the kitchen. His voice showed his humor. "You wanted flowers."

Dropping her bags on the floor without care as to what was in them, she ran down the hall and into his arms, kissing him with all her joy and excitement.

Within seconds her hands were reaching for the buttons on his shirt, as he started unzipping her dress.

An hour later, they lay on their bed, her head resting on his chest. He moved so that he could kiss her hair. "Let me say that I originally planned to woo you with an amazing dinner and champagne."

She continued to stroke his chest, realizing anew how much she loved touching him. "You can woo me with dinner now."

She made her move as he cooked. Sipping her wine, she grinned at him. "So, yes. I want to live with you. But I have some conditions."

He turned so that he could lean against the counter and look at her fully. "Ah, negotiating a contract, one of my favorite things."

"First, I'd like us to live here."

He was a little surprised, and it showed. "Really? That works for me, but that gives you a longer commute."

"That's okay with me."

"Great."

"For right now, I want to keep my house. Not saying I don't think this will work, but I know myself well enough to know that if I rented it or sold it, I'd get anxious."

"Of course."

"I want to keep the standing dinner with Luther on Wednesdays."

"I assumed you would."

"And I hope you would join us for that dinner, whether it's here or at his place."

"Of course." He smiled. "And if there are times that you just want to have dinner with him, without me there, say so."

"I will. And you would need to find me some office space here."

He started to laugh. "I assumed that as well, if you moved here. If we moved to your place, I'd have asked the same."

Delaney looked at him intently. "And here's the big one. Later this fall when it's time to renew my contract at the center, I may want to think about a change."

This was a surprise! "I'll support whatever you want to do."

She played with her wine glass, spinning the stem in her fingers. "I've been quietly doing some consulting and writing for the Gates Foundation, and they've approached me with an offer to do that for them more, which I could do from home or wherever I wanted."

"Wow. Congratulations."

"Thanks." She paused. "And I think, maybe—just maybe— I might want to stop the overnight, and transition into private behavioral practice instead. Possibly later in the fall."

James felt joy blooming in him. He had desperately wanted to ask her to give up the work at Mercy but knew how much it meant to her. "You know I'd love that, but if you change your mind, I'll support you."

She stretched up to wrap her arms around his neck, pulling him down to her. "That was the right answer."

"Do I know how to negotiate or what?"

"I got everything I asked for. What do you want?"

His kiss was sure. "I got everything I wanted when you said yes to living with me."

Chapter Thirty-three

A month later, Delaney couldn't believe how easy the transition had been merging their lives together. No nightmares, or dreams that made her cry with grief in the shower—everything was great.

That afternoon, driving home from work, Delaney stopped to get gas. Getting back into the car, she was startled when her phone went off with a very distinctive tone. Instead of pulling out into traffic, she pulled into a parking space and connected the call. "Hi, Jesse."

"Del. Glad to reach you. How are you?"

"Fine. What's up?" Delaney loved her cousin very much, but their relationship had been hidden from James and from everyone in her New England life except Luther. Usually they communicated by text or email, and made one quick visit a year, usually in Chicago.

"The farm, Del. The farm. You have to make a decision."

"I told you I needed time."

"They've given you the time you asked for! They're offering cash, fair market value, you keep the lake house. It's a fabulous offer. But they're getting antsy, and the lease runs out at the end of the year. They're beginning to mention not staying on the property if they have to keep leasing it."

Delaney could feel anxiety blooming. She didn't want to deal with any of this! It was too much, and it brought her past roaring into her present and possibly her future. "I know, Jess. I get it." She swallowed, trying to think. "Can you ask them to give me two weeks? I'll give them an answer in two weeks, I promise."

"I can try."

Fifteen minutes later, her phone buzzed with a text. *Two weeks, no more. After that, they will pull out of any future lease.*

Delaney pulled into the driveway, glad that James wasn't home yet. He'd gone to a late meeting with the gallery owner and planned to be home in time for dinner.

After putting her bags away, and changing into leggings and a sweatshirt, Delaney started the stew heating, then went to her little office. With a sigh, she opened her laptop and accessed the secure drive. Her heart raced as she looked at the photos of the farm. The land where she'd been born, and where she'd lived until she was eight. For a moment, she could smell the corn stalks, and hear the horses' hooves as the Amish wagons and buggies went down the road. She could hear her little brother screaming with laughter on the tire swing. How many hours had she spent pushing him on that swing? How much she missed him. Did she ever want to go back to the farm? No. She leaned back in the chair, trying to identify her emotions. Did she want to sell it? Maybe, maybe not. It wasn't that she ever wanted to go back there, but if she sold it, it would be the last chapter of that part of her life. Right?

With trembling fingers, she clicked on a photo file. Her heart constricted as she looked at the ancient photo of her with Jacob. If she sold the farm, would she be forgetting Jacob forever? She stared at the picture. "I miss you so much, Jakie."

Just then, she heard the garage door, and knew that James was home. Snapping the computer shut, she tried to regulate her emotions, knowing how attuned he was to her feelings. What the hell was she going to do?

Tomorrow and Yesterday

Chapter Thirty-four

That night, Delaney snuggled into James' arms, trying to will her body into calm. His voice was gentle. "You okay?"

"I'm fine. Why?"

"You've seemed really far away this evening."

She tried to keep the worry from her voice. "No, just tired."

An hour later, James awoke to her screaming, "No! No, please no! Me, get me!"

Sitting up, he pulled her shaking body into his arms. "Laney! Wake up, love, it's just a dream. Wake up!"

Delaney awoke with a start, and as she realized where she was, she knew what must have happened. It had been years since she'd had a nightmare about those final moments! Her dreams usually swirled around that night, but to see Jake again, just as she remembered him from that time…*Damn* it! That was cruel. Why couldn't her past just stay in the past?

She sat up, trying to control her racing heart, hearing it pumping wildly. "I'm okay. Just a dream."

James turned on the bedside light to look at her, seeing how pale she was, and how much she was still shaking. "Tell me about it."

Her eyes were stricken. "Don't worry about it. It was just a dream. Nothing more."

"What do you mean?"

"It was just a dream. It doesn't mean anything. I'm okay."

His voice stayed gentle but was tinged with frustration. "Laney, I love you. You just started screaming in your sleep, something is going on. Talk to me."

Pulling away from him, she drew her knees up to her chest and wrapped her arms around them. "It was a dream about my childhood, okay? I don't want to talk about it. What's done is done."

"Laney, it isn't done if it still impacts you this way." He tried to soften his voice. "If you won't talk to me, how about seeing someone? Maybe too many transitions so soon are impacting you too much."

Fear filled her. Did he not want her in his life anymore? "What are you saying, that you think this is a mistake?"

"Jesus, Laney, no! That's not what I'm saying at all. What I'm saying is that clearly it still bothers you, and maybe with all the life decisions you've made or are making right now, you need some extra support. If you won't let me be that person, then someone else!"

She started to cry. "I love you. Know that. I'm really okay, but I promise I'll reach out if I'm not."

What else could he say? "Fair enough."

Chapter Thirty-five

Just over a week later, she stood in the doorway to the closet holding up two dresses. "Which one?"

James looked up from tying his tie. "The blue."

"Thank you."

He smiled at her in the mirror. "How about we bag it and stay home, then you don't need a dress at all?"

"Your brother and my best friend are announcing their engagement, we need to go!" As she said this, she dropped her robe on the bed, and shrugged into the little dress.

He came up behind her, sliding the zipper up her back. "What about staying here and celebrating ourselves?"

She looked over her shoulder at him, confused. "What are you talking about?"

He came around in front of her, sat on the bed, and took her hands. "Will you marry me?"

The shock made her knees weak, and Delaney steadied herself by putting her hands on his shoulders. "Are you serious?"

"Never more serious." He looked up at her. "Delaney, will you please marry me?"

Her face crumbled. "I…"

Shock filled him. "You don't want to marry me?"

"No! Yes!" She tried to pull her thoughts together. "Jesus, James, *yes* I want to marry you." Her voice trailed off. "But, I can't."

"What are you talking about?"

"I can't marry you unless I can tell you everything. You can't marry me until you know everything, and…" Just then his phone buzzed with the alarm reminding them of the upcoming social event. "We have to go." She rested her forehead on his. "I want to marry you more than anything. I do. But you need to know some things first. Then see if you still want to marry me."

He almost shouted, "I don't care about those things. I want to marry you." He pulled her close to kiss her abdomen. "I want to have children with you. I want to grow old with you. I want us to have the same last name. Damn it, Laney. I love you and I want to marry you."

The alarm sounded again. She tipped his chin up to gaze into his beautiful dark eyes that had grown stormy during the conversation. "Tonight, when we get home, we'll talk. And if it takes all night, so be it. And if after all of that, after you've had time to think, you still want to marry me, then I'll be thrilled to be your wife."

Chapter Thirty-six

At the party, Delaney expressed her joy to Pam, admired the stunning diamond solitaire, hugged Thomas, and sipped a half a glass of champagne she really didn't want. All the while, she tried to keep a smile on her face and not act like her world was crumbling around her. At one point, she realized that she'd been daydreaming about the possibilities of marrying this amazing man, then realized anew that once he knew who she really was, it might all come crashing down around her. Yes, Tom had married her, but that hadn't lasted, and he hadn't known the truth.

Just then, Delaney felt eyes on her, and was horrified when it was clear that someone had asked her a question. Three sets of eyes were blinking as they awaited her response. She choked out the words, "I'm sorry. I think I was daydreaming..." She sent a pleading look at Pam, hoping she'd help her out of the awkward situation. "...about what hellish dress Pam is going to make me wear as her maid of honor."

That sparked a renewed conversation about details for the upcoming wedding, and Delaney could return to her thoughts. Was tonight going to be the night she lost James? For a moment, she felt her throat closing at the thought of losing him, of not waking up each morning beside him, not having him complete her.

Standing nearby, James watched Delaney's face grow paler and paler, and she started rubbing her arms, clearly cold. Looking at his brother Tony, James smiled. "Hey, Tony, it looks like Laney is freezing over there. I'll be back, okay?"

"Of course, Jimmy." He squeezed his little brother's shoulder. "She's amazing, man. So glad you two found each other."

"Me too." James took a couple steps, shrugging out of his blazer as he did so. Reaching Delaney's side, he draped the jacket over her shoulders, wrapping his arm around her as well. "You okay?"

She looked up at him, somewhat dazed. "Yeah. Thank you. I'm freezing."

"You're really pale. Do you feel okay?"

She tipped her head. "I have a headache. That's all. And I'm cold."

James kissed her cheek. "I'll go get your shawl and some Advil. Be right back."

She smiled, much warmer in his huge jacket. "Thank you." She hugged him. "Love you."

"Love you."

Waiting for James to come back, Delaney stood next to Gail watching the milling crowd celebrating Pam and Thomas' engagement. Trying to focus on the event, Delaney tried to reassure herself that everything was going to be okay when she told James. Maybe he would understand and still love her.

Just then an older woman stopped short in front of her. "Delaney? You are Delaney, aren't you? Delaney Perkins?"

Hearing the last word, Delaney's heart constricted, but before she could answer, Gail jumped in with, "Joan! So glad you could make it. Yes, this is Delaney, but not Perkins. Delaney *Adams*, who lives with our James."

The older woman looked shrewdly at Delaney, and Delaney fought the urge to run, feeling her world shatter under her feet. "No, you're Delaney Perkins. I'd know you anywhere. You are the absolute spitting image of your mother, Jane Michaels, then after she married your dad, Jane Perkins. I know who you are."

Just as Delaney opened her mouth to make a lame excuse, James came up beside her, gripping her arm in an iron grasp. "We need to talk now."

Delaney looked at the strange woman, trying to sound as normal as possible. "Please excuse me, I'll be back in just a minute."

Pulled along by James, Delaney followed him into the family library. Once there, James closed the door firmly behind them. "Are you lying to me?"

Delaney was still reeling from the woman's comments, so confused that she didn't know how to respond. She just stared at him, not saying a word.

His voice lowered dangerously, and she realized that she'd never seen him that angry. "Are you lying to me?"

"What are you talking about?"

He pulled her phone from his pocket and shoved it in her face. "Are you having an affair?"

That was the last thing she expected to hear from him! "No! Why would you think that?"

He hit the home button on her phone, and it lit up with text after text from Jesse. Her heart sank as James held the phone in front of her, scrolling down the texts. "Since we've been here, this Jesse has texted you fourteen times. And he's important enough to you that you have a picture of the two of you as the icon for him. And he's telling you that you have to make a decision, one way or the other, that you need to call him, and that he loves you." His voice dropped to almost a whisper, but one that made her blood run cold. "So, I will ask you again, Delaney. And damn it, tell me the truth! Are you having an affair?"

"No! I'm not having an affair."

"Then who the hell is Jesse and why does he have this connection to you? Why is he pushing you to make a decision and what the fuck do you need to decide?"

Without responding, Delaney took three steps backward to sit on the couch behind her. Putting her head in her hands, she choked, "Jesse is my lawyer."

"Bullshit! That's bullshit, Delaney. I'm your damn lawyer. I'm the one who looked over those contracts for you, not him. And if he's just your lawyer, as far-fetched as that sounds, he certainly feels like more when he tells you he loves you."

Her shoulders slumped, and seeing the gesture, for a moment, James felt ashamed of his attack. Taking a deep breath, he strode over to the chair across from the couch. "Talk to me, Laney. If what we have means anything to you, you need to tell me what the hell is going on."

She looked up at him, and the pain on her face made his heart constrict. His voice softened. "Talk to me. Please."

She reached up to twist a strand of hair. "Jesse is my lawyer." She looked down at her hands. "And my cousin."

"Your *cousin*?" His shock was clear.

"My cousin. His mom, who died when we were little, was my mom's sister. He's my only blood relative." She looked up at him. "And he's my lawyer, because I still have property and business interests where he lives, and I don't have anything to do with them, so he takes care of them for me." She gestured toward the phone. "And the decision I need to make is that the farm I was born on has been leased by an Amish family since my family died, but now they want to buy it outright, and if I don't agree to sell it, they're going to pull out of leasing it, and then I'll have this huge piece of property I hate that I'll have to deal with…"

He came over, taking her hand in his. "I don't understand, Delaney. Why the secrecy? You say you want to marry me, but I don't know anything about where you're from, I don't know anything about your biological family. It's like before you arrived at Brown, you didn't exist. Please help me understand."

Just then her phone lit up again, and she saw in dismay that it was Jesse. The text was brief: *Call me now!!!!!*

Delaney flipped the phone over. "He can wait." She looked up at James. "Jesse is my cousin, he's six months older than I am. After my mom died, his dad didn't want anything to do with me or my family. But he did. So, we found ways to stay connected, and as adults, he became my lawyer, and he takes care of the details there…"

"Where? Where the hell are we talking about, Delaney? I don't even know that." His face showed his pain. "I proposed to you tonight, and I don't even know where you're from."

"Indiana. A little town outside of Fort Wayne. Amish country."

"Continue."

"Once a year, we get together somewhere for a visit, usually Chicago. He's married now and has two great kids, so we meet someplace for a weekend. He's my friend, my only relative, and my advisor. He takes care of my properties, and all that stuff for me."

"Your properties? Like your house here?"

"No. I paid cash for the house, and it's separate from my financial holdings in Indiana."

"Okay."

Her phone buzzed again with a text, which she ignored. He shook his head. "Go ahead and check it."

She flipped it over and saw, *I need to talk to you now, Del. Call me!*

"I'll call him in a bit." She looked at him, waiting for him to continue.

"Properties? What are we talking here?"

She rubbed her arms, feeling the chill seep into her bones. "I own the farm."

"How big of a farm?"

"Six hundred acres. Most of it used for soybeans and corn."

"Jesus."

"The house I lived in is gone, but they built a small house on the property. Three big barns, one for the livestock, one for the equipment, one now for storage. It's rented by an Amish family who owns the adjoining property."

"And that's it?"

"No."

"Tell me, please."

"I own a lake house in Indiana, with ten acres of land on the lake. And a restaurant in the town where I lived. I used to own a string of car dealerships, but I sold those years ago." She sighed, ill at ease with the topic at hand. "And there's a foundation that does social justice work, primarily around domestic abuse, that I established with some of what I inherited."

Shock filled him as pieces started to come together. "The Del Foundation? That's *you*?"

"It is."

He stood up, going to the window, staring unseeingly at the trees outside. "You're behind the Del Foundation?" he repeated.

"I am. Well, no, I'm not really. The money I inherited funds it, along with the money from the dealerships, and I still guide funding priorities, but it's all done without my identity being known."

James' head was whirling. He turned to look at her. "I don't know what to say, Laney. This is a hell of a lot of information to take in at once."

"I know. That's why I said we needed to talk tonight, that you need to decide after you know it all if you want to marry me."

"Of course I want to marry you, I just, wow. It's a lot to take in."

Her phone started to ring, and James shook his head. "Answer it, clearly it's important."

Delaney picked up the phone, swiping the screen. "Jesse, I can't talk right now. I'll call you later."

As she started to hit the end button, James heard a male voice yell, "Del, don't hang up, it's Jeanine!"

As James watched in fascination, her face went pure white and she clutched at the phone convulsively. "What do you mean?"

His voice was so loud that James could hear him say clearly, "Del, she had a heart attack this afternoon. I just got word a while ago, and I'm on my way there now. But it's bad, Del, bad. She's in critical condition in the ICU at Lutheran. You need to get here, now, Del, before it's too late."

Tears started spilling down her cheeks, and James could see her shaking violently as he moved to take her into his arms, caring about nothing more than comforting her. The rest of the discussion could wait.

Through her sobs, she choked out, "I'll find a flight there, and get to the hospital. Keep sending me updates, and I'll get there as soon as I can."

"Fine. When you get a flight, text Anna, and she'll pick you up at the airport."

"I will." Her voice broke. "I love you, Jess."

"Love you too."

"You tell her that I love her and to hold on."

"I will. See you soon."

Disconnecting the call, she dropped the phone on the couch and fell into James' arms, sobbing. As she tried to speak, he couldn't understand what she was saying so he finally just whispered, "Laney, it's okay. I understand. We're going to Indiana. We'll figure this out, love." As he rocked her, he just kept saying, "We'll go to Indiana, love. It's okay."

Finally, his words made it to her brain. Her voice showed her shock. "You'll go with me?"

"Absolutely!"

Tears were still streaking her pale face as she reached up to cradle his, kissing him. His lips were gentle, and she felt her world beginning to make sense again. She grabbed her phone. "I need to find a flight to Fort Wayne."

"No, you don't." He kissed the tip of her nose. "I'll be right back. Take a breather and I'll be right back." He paused. "I assume Luther knows everything?"

"He does. He figured it out years ago."

"He's a damn fine detective…"

Ten minutes later, when he hadn't returned, Delaney cautiously left the library, walking back to the party, trying to find her equilibrium. As she came into the room, she heard Gail hissing at the woman who had confronted her earlier. "I will tell you again, Joan. Delaney is not Delaney *Perkins*. Period. And if you insist on bringing this up, I'll ask you to leave."

Just then, James came up beside Delaney, putting a steadying hand on her back. Delaney took a deep breath, looked up at him, and whispered, "I'm sorry, I wanted to tell you this first, but I need to do this." Taking a deep breath, she stepped forward. "Gail. Wait a minute, please." She looked at the other woman. "Joan, yes, I'm Delaney Perkins, although I changed my name legally many years ago. But yes, you're right." Her lips trembled. "And maybe someday we could get together and you could tell me about my mom. I don't remember her that well anymore."

The guests were stunned. There were very few people alive who didn't know the name Delaney Perkins. Everyone started talking at once.

James pulled Delaney into his protective arms, and guided her away from the crowd, back to the library. Once the door was closed, and he had thrown the lock on the door, he turned to her, holding out his arms. She sagged against him, needing his love and his warmth. He kissed her hair. "So, love of mine, are we done with surprises for tonight?"

She tried to laugh, although he could see tears forming. "I hope so." She looked at him, her face a mask of pain. "I am so sorry, James. I wanted to tell you when it was just us. I'm so sorry that you found out this way." Her voice broke. "I understand if this is too much for you."

His voice was stern. "You listen to me. I loved you before, I love you still. That doesn't change. And now we need to get you to Indiana as soon as possible. While I was out there, I talked to Dad, and he has the company jet fueling right now. We're going to leave right now, go to the house, and meet Luther there because I thought it might help for you to see him for a few minutes. We'll get a few things, and get to Green, and then we'll be in Fort Wayne in under four hours."

"You mean it?"

"Absolutely."

Chapter Thirty-seven

Luther met them at the house, giving Delaney a long hug. Within minutes, they were on the road again, headed to the airport, Delaney not having seen the file that Luther handed James.

Once the plane was underway, James looked at Delaney, and saw the absolute exhaustion on her face. "It was Jesse asking you about the farm decision that sparked your nightmare?"

"Probably."

He motioned to the back of the small jet. "You could go take a nap, love. A couple hours sleep would do a lot right now."

She shook her head. "No. I'll stay here." She pulled the blanket the attendant had given her over her lap. "I can sleep here."

"That works too." James waited while she reclined her seat as far as it could go, then curled up on her side. He covered her fully with the soft blanket, tucking it in around her. Within minutes, she'd fallen into an exhausted sleep. When she was finally sleeping, he motioned for the attendant to bring him a stiff drink.

As he sipped his drink, he watched Delaney sleep. His Delaney was *Delaney Perkins*? What he could remember of the case from his law school days, simply put, she had lived through hell. How could she be so well-adjusted, happy, and full of love with what she had endured? The urge to protect her and give her joy swelled in him, and he realized he was gripping his glass tighter than needed.

With one more sip, he opened the file Luther had slipped him. Inside, there was a note on yellow legal paper.

James,

When I met Delaney her first week of college, I knew there was more to her story than she was telling. Yes, I dug until I had put it together. She knows I know it all, but she has never seen this full file. It is up to you if you want to share it with her.

Thank you for loving her – Luther

The first images made him almost drop his heavy glass. The photos were of the crime scene, and he looked in horror as he saw her pregnant mother and little brother, lying dead in pools of blood on the kitchen floor. The next were of her father, dead on the front porch from a self-inflicted gunshot wound.

He took another sip of the whisky. He'd learned about the case. *Every* law student had learned about the case at some point. But it had been just an academic exercise then, not the story of the woman he loved. Just then, she stirred in her sleep, and he gently stroked her hair until she calmed.

Pushing aside the photos, he turned to the written report. As he read page after page, his heart ached for the woman beside him, who clearly had been denied any childhood at all.

"Upon review, it was clear that a few community members had raised concerns about the issues at the Perkins' house. Ms. Jeanine Adams, kindergarten and first grade teacher, had

made six known reports to Child Protective Services, but the reports were never taken for investigation. Upon further review, records showed that Ms. Adams was removed from her job at Hope Valley Primary School, due to supposed budgetary cuts, although her position was filled just prior to the next school year. The administrative assistant to Principal Chambers gave a sworn statement that Ms. Adams was non-renewed because she continued to report the suspected abuse of Delaney Perkins to authorities, and that the local authorities did not want to investigate her father, a well-known businessman and member of the town council."

James read that paragraph over and over. This had to be the Jeanine they were going to see. This woman had sacrificed her career to try to save little Delaney.

He continued reading.

"The neighbors, Mr. and Mrs. Ebersole reported that they often would hear Mr. Perkins yelling and swearing at his wife and children, often seeming to focus most of his rage on Delaney. When it would get very heated, Delaney would often antagonize her father and run from the house, running for the corn fields, and he would follow her, trying to find her to punish her. They reported that often, due to his level of intoxication, he would stumble and fall in the fields, and pass out. Sometimes he would find her, and that they suspected the punishment was severe. They said that often when he passed out, they would go out later that night, and find Delaney in their horse barn, hiding. Mrs. Ebersole reported that on Delaney's seventh birthday there was an especially ugly night, and that she found Delaney hidden in the barn in the early hours of the next day. She reported that Delaney said that if

she made her father angry at her, and he followed her into the fields, then he wouldn't hurt her mother or brother."

James stopped, his heart clenching. A little girl had knowingly antagonized her abuser to get him to go after her, luring him out into the fields, to spare her mother and brother. Who was protecting *her*?

Then he turned to the next page, and his heart fell.

"On the day of the murders, the Ebersoles reported hearing yelling much of the day. They said that they could hear Mr. Perkins yelling about how Delaney wasn't sick, and she needed to go to school. At one point, they reported that Mr. and Mrs. Perkins were out on the porch, and he was yelling that Delaney was faking being sick, and that Mrs. Perkins was to take her to school, and go back to work at the restaurant, that he wasn't going to pay for others to work at the restaurant while she stayed home with 'the faker' Delaney. Mrs. Perkins kept yelling that Delaney had a fever, and that the school would not allow her to come back until she'd been fever free for twenty-four hours. Finally, she said that he could go back to work, and that she would take Delaney back to school, and go to the restaurant. He said that he would see her at the restaurant in thirty minutes. After he drove away, Mrs. Perkins went to the Ebersole farm, and asked it Delaney could just rest in their barn..."

James re-read that last part of the sentence over and over. Her mother was so afraid of her husband that she asked the neighbors to hide Delaney in the *barn* when she was sick. The *barn*. Jesus Christ. A baby, not much older than his nephew Devon, was hidden in a *barn* when she was sick because her mother was afraid of her father, and her father was insisting the child go back to school! He picked up the file again.

"… and that she would be back for her when the restaurant closed for the day. They agreed, and Mrs. Ebersole brought her a blanket and juice to the barn.

"That afternoon, Mrs. Perkins returned, and as she was walking Delaney from the barn to the car, Mr. Perkins pulled into his driveway and saw them. They reported that he stood there, glaring at his pregnant wife and daughter, said, 'Get in the house now!' and then walked into the house, slamming the door behind him."

In horror, James put the pieces together. When Delaney had been so sick, she had said that others suffered if she stayed home sick, and that the last time she had done so, she'd been eight. Holy shit!

He continued reading.

"On the night of the murders, Mr. and Mrs. Ebersole reported that Mr. Perkins had been shouting for more than an hour, several windows had been broken, and that they could hear Mrs. Perkins yelling at him to stop, begging him to leave them alone. They called 9-1-1 at 7:32 p.m. to report the disturbance, but the police did not respond until almost an hour later, at 8:19, after shots had been fired. They also reported that after Mrs. Perkins had been heard begging him to leave them alone, they could hear Delaney yelling at him to stop hurting them, to come get her, just to get her, and called him an asshole. They heard Delaney yelling on the front lawn, and their son reported seeing her head among the rows of corn, screaming at her father to be a man and come get her, not them.

When the police arrived, Jane Perkins, her unborn daughter, and son Jacob were found dead from multiple gunshot wounds. Mr. Perkins was found dead of a self-inflicted gunshot wound to the head, the weapon still in his hands. Delaney was nowhere to be found.

Eight-year-old Delaney Perkins was found late in the afternoon on the next day, hidden in the corn, hypothermic, dehydrated, and delusional. When taken to the hospital, she was found to have a skull fracture, a broken rib, and eighteen healed broken bones. The skull fracture was new, and doctors felt that the fracture was inflicted that night, prior to her run into the field."

James flipped to the next page and saw photo after photo of the x-rays taken in the days after she was admitted to the hospital. Having been a public prosecutor, he'd seen his share of horrific abuse pictures, but he had to admit these were the worst that he'd ever seen. How had she survived?

The next page was a summary from Child Protective Services:

"Following her release from the hospital, Delaney was placed into a state foster home, as no relatives stepped forward to take guardianship. Over the three years, Delaney was in seventeen separate foster homes. Each family reported that she was recalcitrant, almost mute, refused to take part in religious observances, and would not accept normal punishment for misbehavior. She also ran away more than twenty times from the foster homes, and each time was found by the police. Several times she was on the run for more than two days; once, when she was eleven, she was on the run for nine days.

At eleven, the state made the decision to place Delaney in the Walfin Home for Children, in hopes that their rigid attention to schedule and behavioral expectations would force Delaney into socially acceptable behavior.

On the day Delaney was being transported (in handcuffs) to her new placement, Ms. Jeanine Adams came forward and stated that she would adopt Delaney. Delaney's adoption was finalized on the day before her twelfth birthday."

Chapter Thirty-eight

James realized he was being watched and looked down to see Delaney's blue eyes looking at him warily. She glanced at the paper in front of him, and said guardedly, "Wow. That's a walk down memory lane."

She adjusted her seat, then sat up, and James watched as she pulled into as small of a shape as possible, her arms going around herself protectively. James could see how vulnerable she felt and for a moment, he was filled with remorse for reading the file. He carefully closed it, setting it down on the tray, shifting so he was looking straight at her.

Her tone was hostile. "Luther gave you his file?"

"He did."

"And you didn't think that maybe you should have asked me if I was okay with you reading it?" Her eyes swam with tears. "That maybe, right now, going on this trip, might not be the time I'd most like you to read this?"

He put out his hands, hoping that she would take them. When she didn't, he reached down to touch her knee, seeing her visibly flinch as he touched her. "I was wrong to do it, Laney." He looked at her intently, trying to make her understand. "I knew the rough details about it, just about any law student in the U.S. studies the case, but yes, Luther gave me the file, and I should've asked you if you were okay with me reading it."

He could see how rigid her body was. "I know everyone knows the story, or thinks they do, but…"

"But what?"

"You love me. Waking up, seeing you reading it, seeing those pictures of the x-rays, it makes me feel like a zoo animal." Tears streamed down her cheeks. "I felt like a zoo animal every single day after it happened, until I came to Brown. I was able to start new there, no one whispered about it, about me. And you reading it makes me feel that way." She started to shake. "I already feel like I'm going back into that zoo cage by going to Indiana, but for Jeanine, I'd do anything."

James opened his arms. "Please come here, Laney, please. I love you. I was wrong."

She stared at him, and in horror, James watched as she shook her head. "I can't, James, I can't. I feel too vulnerable as it is. I know that I should've told you all this before now, but how you and Luther could do this without asking me how I felt about it?" She stood up, dropping the blanket on the seat. "I'm going to the bathroom, and right now, I need some time, some space."

"Laney, stop!"

"I can't." She could feel the pressure building in her ears. "I think we're descending. I need to get my head on straight, and I can't do it trying to make things right with us." She looked at him. "I understand that you probably feel I'm overreacting, but I need you to take a step back."

She walked away, shutting and locking the door to the small bathroom behind her.

When she returned, she sat down across from him, noticing that the file was nowhere to be seen. "I'd like the file, please."

He pulled it from his bag and handed it to her silently. She took it, reached over to tuck it in her own bag, and said, "Thank you."

"You're welcome." He looked at her with sad eyes. "What does taking a step back mean? What is it that you want—what you need—from me?"

She leaned back, buckling her seat belt, then looked at him seriously. "It means that either you're going to head back home, or if you're staying, I need you to give me some space. It's all I can do to keep myself somewhat regulated with the idea that I'm about to land in Indiana for the first time since I left for college, and that one of the people I love most in the world is struggling to live. I know what you did, you did from a place of love, but right now, I feel really violated, and I need to focus on Jeanine, not us right now. If you stay, I need you to understand that I don't know if I want to share a bed with you tonight, and that I don't want you to touch me right now."

"I can do that." He leaned on the tray, wishing he could just hold her. "I love you. I was wrong, and I know it, and I get that this is too much right now."

"Thank you."

Landing at the airport, they walked to the car rental desk. Handing over her identification, Delaney told the clerk that they both would be driving the car. When they got to the rented car, James said, "I'll drive."

"No, I know the way. It's easier if I do."

Clearly, she'd made up her mind. "Okay."

Getting in the car, Delaney connected her phone to Bluetooth, and called Jesse. "Hey."

"Hey. You here?"

"Yeah, we just landed, and are in the car."

"Anna would've come to get you."

"I know, but this way we have our own vehicle, so you guys aren't stuck driving us around."

"Fine. And you have reservations at the Hilton."

"Thank you." Her voice was suddenly shaky. "How is she?"

"Holding on. She drifts in and out. The nurses feel that when I told her you were on the way, that she seemed to settle down some." He said something to someone on his end. "Del, go check in, get a couple hours of sleep, and I'll meet you at the hospital at nine tomorrow morning. We can't get in to see her until then. They'll call me if something changes."

"Okay."

Silently, Delaney drove through the dark streets, finally pulling in under the portico of the Fort Wayne Hilton. Handing the keys and a tip to the valet, they got out of the car. Delaney reached into the trunk for her bags, but James reached in over her hand. "I've got them."

For a moment, she wanted to argue, but realized how tired she was. "Fine."

Ten minutes later, James used the keycard to open the door to their room. Two beds stared back at them. Letting Delaney enter first, James dropped their bags on the couch. Delaney gestured toward the bathroom. "I'm going to take a quick shower."

"Of course." He didn't know what to do. "Would you like something to eat?"

She rubbed her forehead. "I don't know."

Keeping his physical distance, James looked at her. "Laney, why don't I order something, and if you want some, eat it?"

"Okay."

While Delaney showered, James ordered a bottle of wine, a tossed salad, and a pizza. She came out dressed in her favorite leggings, a hoodie, and thick socks. When she smelled the food, her stomach growled loudly.

"Hungry?"

"I am." She looked down at her feet. "Thank you for ordering something."

"You're welcome."

They sat across from each other at the small table, and James was pleased when she nodded yes when he gestured toward the wine. She pulled a piece of pizza off the tray and added some salad to the plate. James did the same.

After a couple of bites in complete silence, Delaney pushed her salad around her plate with her fork. Her voice was low. "I'm not mad at you. I just need to figure this all out."

"I know."

They ate the rest of the meal in silence. When done, Delaney stood and picked up the remains, and James knew she needed to move to release her pent-up anxiety. His eyes widened in shock when she went to her bag and pulled out the familiar file, bringing it back to the table.

She sat down across from him and opened the file on the table. His voice was strained. "Laney, don't do this. You don't have to do this."

She looked at him, and for the first time since he'd met her, her eyes lacked all emotion. "I *do* need to do this." In silence, she read Luther's note, then read page after page of the report. Feeling trapped, James sat equally quiet on the other side of the table, trying to gauge her emotions. When she got to the pile of photos of the x-rays, he saw her swallow hard.

Her voice dead calm, she placed photo after photo on the table, spread out. She pointed to the first one, where her lower arm had been broken. "My fifth birthday." Then she indicated one showing a broken rib on her left side and said, "New Year's Eve when I was six." She explained another where two ribs on her right side were fractured by saying, "When I tried to stop him on Jacob's fourth birthday, I was seven." In that same detached voice, she sifted through the photos, and James' heart constricted with pain, hearing her recount the dates or events of each of the breaks. When it came to the film of her skull fracture, she paused. "I've never seen this one before. That was the night he killed them."

She looked at James and he could see the raw pain in her eyes. "My mom told him she was leaving. He had hit her, hit all of us again, the night before. It was getting more frequent, and he'd been trying to hit her stomach. She told him she was leaving him before he killed the baby. I remember him screaming that he would kill her before he'd let her leave him. And when he went after her, Jacob and I tried to stop him. He backhanded Jacob across the room, and he just huddled there, crying for him to stop. I remember I kicked him, and he grabbed me by my dress." She looked blindly past him. "I was wearing this yellow dress. He grabbed me by the front of it and basically threw me. I hit my head on the table; I remember it made me dizzy. I was really sick, and had felt dizzy all day, probably from the fever, but the knock to my head made it hard to see. But he was going after my mom again, so I remember getting up, and yelling at him that he wasn't man enough to get me, that he was an asshole, and I took off for the fields. Usually he would chase me to teach me a lesson. Sometimes he would find me. Sometimes he would fall and pass out. No matter what, it meant that Mom and Jacob got left alone." She rubbed her forehead. "But he didn't follow me…"

James ached to hold her. "Laney, I am so sorry. I don't know what to say. It's hard to comprehend."

"I know." She almost smiled. "It's hard to think about it. It was so long ago, and I've worked so hard to keep the firewall in place, but now it's like re-experiencing it all over again."

"What can I do to help?"

"I don't know." She gathered the pages together and put them back in the file. She stood up and placed the file in front of him. "You can have it back."

"I don't want or need it back."

"Neither do I." She walked away, heading into the bathroom, and moments later, James could hear the familiar sounds of her brushing her teeth.

When she came out, she walked over toward the beds, then stopped, clearly hesitating. With her back to him, she said, "James, I love you."

"I love you too."

"I know you do." She turned around to gaze at him seriously. "I need to sleep in a different bed from you tonight. Please understand, I need to get myself okay in my own head, and touching you is just going to make it worse right now."

It was one of the last things he wanted her to say, but he was relieved to hear that she loved him still. "I understand." He sighed. "Laney, would you prefer that I see if there's another room for me tonight?"

"No!" Her shoulders fell. "I can't sleep next to you tonight, but I can't bear the thought of you not being near." Her eyes swam with unshed tears. "I know this sounds weird."

"No, it doesn't. I get it." He stood up. "I'm going to take a shower. You get into bed, watch TV if you want, and then let's get as much sleep as we can. Tomorrow is likely to be a long day."

"Okay."

When he came back out after his shower, the lights were all out except for the small bedside table lamp next to his bed. He could see her huddled up under the covers, still wearing her sweatshirt. He climbed under the comforter and reached out to turn off the light. "Night, Laney. Love you."

"Love you."

Later, he awoke to soft sounds coming from the bed next to his. Disoriented at first, he realized that the sounds were from Delaney crying. His heart ached for her, and all he wanted was to go take her in his arms and hold her. "Laney, I'm here."

"I know." She sniffed. "It helps, thank you."

Chapter Thirty-nine

The next morning, James was amazed as he watched Delaney drive through Fort Wayne without using the GPS. Pulling into the drive at the hospital, she paused, looked for the garage, and found a spot.

In the lobby, she quickly got directions to the ICU, and hurried there. After checking in with the nurses' desk, she walked down the hall, James behind her, until she came to the right room. James saw her hands shake as she opened the door.

A feeble voice was barely audible. "I told you to never look back."

As James watched in fascination, Delaney stood up straight, her hands balled into fists, and said in a strident voice, "And I told you if I was going to do that, you needed to take care of yourself, which clearly you didn't do! So, don't give me shit, old woman."

A man James recognized as Jesse stood up from the chair next to the bed, laughing. "All right you two, new record. Less than five seconds, and you're already going at it." He held out his arms, and Delaney hugged him hard, then he turned. "You must be James."

"I am." They shook hands.

Delaney took a cautious step toward the bed. The small form under the blanket looked very fragile, but the dark eyes that were laser focused on Delaney looked anything but weak. Delaney swallowed, then said in a tiny voice, "Hi."

"Hi." Her voice stayed brusque. "Well, if you're here, you might as well come give me a hug."

Delaney swept forward, her hands reaching for Jeanine's, holding them as she started to cry. Leaning down, Delaney kissed her cheek.

Jeanine looked lovingly at her. "Lovey, don't cry. I'm going to be fine, and now you're here." Pulling her IV tube with her, she reached up a hand and put it on the side of Delaney's face. "Let me look at you." She pointed at a chair. "Sit down. And then introduce me to your young man." Delaney sat automatically, looked at James, and her smile trembled. "Jeanine, this is James. James, this is Jeanine."

Jeanine looked at him shrewdly. "Nice to meet you. At some point, I will kick these two out of the room, and you and I will talk."

He grinned, liking her immediately. "I look forward to it."

Jeanine looked at the two men. "You two, get out. Go get food or something and let me have some time with my girl."

Sitting at a small table, coffee in front of them, Jesse looked at James. "I'm going out on a limb here, but I suspect you learned everything in the last couple days."

Taking a sip, James nodded. "Yeah. Laney had a nightmare a couple days ago, first one I'd seen her have. She wouldn't talk about it other than to say it was about her childhood. Then, long story short, I proposed, and she said we needed to talk. We were planning on talking anyway last night after a family event, but a woman confronted her calling her Delaney Perkins, then all hell broke loose."

"Sounds like quite an evening..."

"Then on the flight here, she was asleep, and Luther…" He looked at Jesse. "You know Luther?"

"I know *of* him."

"Luther gave me his file on Delaney's early life. As I was reading it, she woke up and saw it, and has since shut down on me completely."

"Ouch."

"Yeah." His shoulders slumped. "She told me that she felt violated by my reading it without asking her, and that I needed to give her space while we were here."

Jesse leaned back in his chair. "I love my cousin. She's one of the bravest, fiercest, most loyal, smartest women I've ever known. Some days she scares the shit out of me with how amazing she is. And most of the time, she can keep all the balls in the air, but right now, this is a lot."

James figured he should get what information he could. "Clearly Jeanine adores her. Why did she send her away?"

"Because she was a walking freak show. People whispered about her all the time, comments were made, people kept watching for her to snap like her dad. And even when they weren't, she perceived they were. She got in more fights in high school than anyone else. Jeanine felt that she needed to get out of here for good, go where she wouldn't face it every day, where there weren't the constant reminders."

"Were people really talking about her that much?"

"They were. Some was well-intentioned, like people telling her that they were sorry that her family was gone. For some, it was curiosity, asking nosy questions like 'had she heard the shots?' For others, it was trying to get her going, get her riled up. By high school, everyone knew she had a short fuse. There were some assholes who would make comments just to see her get mad."

"Jesus."

"Then there were the religious do-gooders. They were constantly telling her they were praying for her, for the souls of her mother, sister, and brother—and praying for her father. She would tell them off." He started to chuckle. "She told the pastor of the Ebenezer Baptist Church, the biggest mega church around, to go fuck himself after he told her that he was praying for her. After her comment, he then said he was praying that God would help her soul see the light so that she wouldn't face eternal damnation like her dad. She tried to slug him, got dragged out of the tent at the fair, and was taken home by police cruiser one more time."

This was so much for James to take in, to think of calm, restrained, almost shy Delaney, who had been so self-contained about dating him, moving in with him, and becoming lovers. To think of her being hauled home by the police? "One more time?"

"Yeah. When she was in foster homes she would run away, and the police picked her up a lot. When Jeanine adopted her, she still showed the old flight or fight response, and if she couldn't get away, she came out swinging. For a small woman, she fought like a demon."

"Really?"

"Yup. And Jeanine didn't give up. Del would punch somebody, get suspended, and Jeanine would make her work during her suspension, ground her, put up with her griping about rules, and gradually she calmed down with love and consistency. By our senior year of high school, I think she only got suspended once, and she was the valedictorian."

"Wow."

"And then they decided she was going to Brown, like her mom, but not using her birth name. Jeanine convinced her that if she went, she needed to go and not look back. She had the properties here, which Jeanine, and later Jeanine and I, took care of and managed, and Del made a new life in the East. The only person out there that eventually knew anything was Luther."

"And you were okay with this?"

"Look, it wasn't my place to be okay with it or not. I didn't have the life she did, and my father abandoned her too, so Jeanine was all she had. I hated to see her leave, but I agreed with Jeanine that it was the only way she could be free. We kept in touch, and over the years, we have actually been in contact more rather than less."

"Okay."

Jesse looked at his watch. "They're going to kick her out in a bit, so we better go back up."

As they came around the corner, they could hear raised voices in the hallway. Jesse stepped forward. "Shit..."

James watched in fascination as Delaney stood toe to toe with a large male nurse who towered over her. Her tone was hostile although she wasn't yelling. "And I understand your rules, but I'm telling you that she says it helps to have me in the room, and so I'm not leaving."

"Visiting hours are clearly posted."

"I don't care where they're posted. I'm going back in there, and I'm sitting with her. You have an issue with it, call security." With that, she turned on her heel, and walked back into Jeanine's room.

The nurse looked at Jesse in frustration, recognizing him at once. "She has to leave."

He shrugged. "She won't."

"But the hospital rules..."

"Call her doctor and have him come over."

"He's not on duty right now, but Dr. Mitchell is."

"Then call Dr. Mitchell."

Jesse and James walked back in the hospital room, and saw Delaney sitting with a stubborn look on her face. "I'm not moving."

Jesse laughed. "Del, I'm not stupid enough to tell you that you have to move. They're calling the doctor."

Just then the door pushed open and a wry voice said, "I should've fucking known it would be you, Del, making the scene."

Delaney looked at the young female doctor in shock. "Beth?"

"Del?" The doctor opened her arms, and Delaney hugged her tightly. "It's so good to see you. When I saw Jeanine's name on the roster, I figured you'd show at some point." She looked over her shoulder. "Hey, Jesse." Her eyes widened, seeing James. "And *hello*! Who are you?"

"James McDaniels."

Laney stepped closer to him, but still didn't touch him. "He's with me."

"Nice to meet you." She paused. "The artist?"

"Yes."

"I saw a show of your work in Chicago last year. Beautiful stuff."

"Thank you."

Dr. Mitchell strode over to the bedside. "Hi Jeanine."

"Bethie." Even exhausted and weak, Jeanine's face showed how amused she was by the situation.

"So, Del here is making a scene that she won't leave your side. Now as I see it, I have two options. One is to get security in here to haul her ass out of here for causing a scene in my hospital and making it so you have to bail her out again." She chuckled. "As much as it would be a walk down memory lane to watch you post bail for her, my bosses might not like it."

"True." Jeanine tried to smile, although she was clearly tiring. "And I'm not really up to that right now."

"Or I can say that she can stay, with a guest if she wants, for the next two hours. Then, we need to do some tests, clean you up, etc. so I'd need to kick her out for a bit, then she could come back later." She was looking directly at Jeanine, but her words were clearly for Delaney. "If she upsets you, and if your vitals change for the worse, I'll haul her out of this room myself."

"Sounds like a plan."

Delaney sat back down with relief. "Thank you."

"You're welcome." She grinned at her. "And before you skip town again, I'd love to sit and visit for a bit. I've missed you."

Delaney's eyes sparkled with tears. "I'd like that."

Ten minutes later, Jesse left with the promise of coming back later that evening. Delaney had moved her chair next to Jeanine, holding her hand silently as the older woman slept. James sat in the chair on the other side of the bed, not saying a word.

Delaney didn't look at him, but whispered, "Thank you."

He looked across the bed, seeing the slash of color on her cheeks that revealed she was emotional. "For what?"

"For coming with me. For loving me. For…"

He waited.

"For not arguing with me when I needed space."

"You're welcome. And I'm so sorry, Laney. I didn't think. I didn't really understand the magnitude of what this all meant to you. I just wanted to understand as quickly as I could, and this seemed like the best way."

"I know." She looked down at her hand, clasping that of the sleeping woman. "Thank you also for not leaving when I told you that you could."

"I'm not leaving you. Period. I blew it, I know that now. I've learned more in the last eight or so hours than I can fathom right now, but I know my life is with you. And I need your help in knowing how to not fuck this up." He tried to find the right words. "I had such a different childhood than yours, I can only understand some of this in an academic way. I need your help in telling me what you need."

"I need you." She finally looked up at him, her eyes serious. "I never thought I'd come back here again, but now that I'm here, I actually know that I need to keep some connection to this place." She looked over at Jeanine. "She's so important to me, and I always kept an eye on her, made sure she was okay, but I love her. I would rather deal with whispers here and be able to have her in my—" She looked at him. "—in our lives."

"We'll figure it out." He smiled at her, feeling more hopeful than he had all day. "We have the rest of our lives to figure it out."

Chapter Forty

The next two days passed in a blur. They spent as much time as they could with Jeanine, including one memorable hour when Jeanine kicked Delaney out of the room so she could interrogate James. She might have been weak physically, but James had to admit that he'd never seen a lawyer question someone as thoroughly as she questioned him. And by the time they were done, he realized that he absolutely adored her too.

By the second night in the hotel, Delaney looked at James, her eyes dark, and said, "Can we sleep in the same bed, but not…" Her cheeks turned bright red. "I love you, I want to be with you, but I'm still too fucked up to…"

He held out his hand, happy when she slipped hers in his. "Of course we can. If you want, I will stay on my side, you stay on yours."

"Thank you."

On the morning of the third day, Delaney's phone rang before dawn, while they were still in bed. Detangling herself from James' limbs, she answered it and heard Jeanine's voice. "They finally let me use a damn phone."

Delaney sat up, any nerves about who was calling replaced by amusement about the comment and tone. "Morning, Jeanine. Feeling better?"

"I am." Her voice became no-nonsense. "I love you, and I want to see you, but you have two things you need to do today instead of coming to see me."

"Anything."

"You know better than to say that to me."

Delaney laughed. "I do. What do you want?"

"You need to go to the farm this morning and make your decision. Then, I need you to go open the restaurant for lunch. I said you'd be there by ten, so chop-chop, Del. Move it."

"Why do you need me to open the restaurant? You have workers."

"They don't own the place. You and I do. And this is the first day it's been open since I got sick. And you'll need to make today's special."

Delaney gritted her teeth. "Fine. What am I making?"

"It's Monday. What do you think you're making?"

Delaney erupted. "No! I am not making it. I swear to God, Jeanine, you did this on purpose. You're getting me back by having me make it."

James rolled over and stroked her back, speaking over her shoulder toward the phone. "Good morning, Jeanine. What are we making?"

Delaney answered in irritation. "Meatloaf. We're making fucking meatloaf. I hate making meatloaf. I hate eating meatloaf. I hate everything to do with meatloaf."

Jeanine laughed. "And it's the Monday special. Get moving and I love you. Call me if you don't remember the recipe."

"Love you too. I hate meatloaf, but I love you."

Delaney put on the blinker to turn into a long driveway. "This is it…"

"Are you okay?"

"No." She stopped a little way in, corn on both sides of the drive. "I never thought I'd see it again."

"You don't have to, love. You can make the decision without coming here."

"No. It's time. Once and for all, it's time."

They pulled up beside a huge red barn. Her voice was low as she said, "The house used to be there, before it was torn down." Beyond that barn were two more barns. Getting out of the car, James could see how nervous Delaney was.

A man about their age in Amish dress came out to meet them. The man looked at the car, then at Delaney. His eyes widened in shock, then he dropped the basket in his hands, and shouted. "Del! Is that you?"

Delaney's face creased in a huge smile, and she dropped her purse in the dirt, jumping forward to run toward the man. "Josiah!"

The two of them shared an extended hug, and as James walked toward them, Delaney took the man's hand, pulling him forward. "Josiah Ebersole, this is James McDaniels. James, this is my friend Josiah." She gestured around. "He's been living here on the farm."

Josiah shook James' hand. "He's your husband?"

Delaney shoved his arm. "Josiah! Stop it."

James grinned. "No, just trying to be."

"How so?"

"I proposed but she hasn't said yes yet." He looked at the barns. "She said she needed to get things here settled first."

Just then an older man stepped from the barn. As he came closer, his mouth curved in a slow smile. "Delaney."

"Simon." Delaney stepped toward him. "It's good to see you again."

For a moment, pain crossed his face. "It has been far too long child." He chuckled. "No one is looking. Come child," he said as he gave her a quick hug. "Welcome home." He then looked at James. "And you are?"

Josiah answered, "James, her intended."

"Congratulations." Simon nodded. "It will be good to see her married properly. From what we heard; your first husband was a snake." He raised an eyebrow. "Besides, you aren't getting any younger, child, and you have a good dowry."

Delaney was horrified, and James tried hard to hide his smile. "Simon! Stop!"

"It's all true." He snorted. "Fine. Want to take a walk?"

The four of them walked around the property, and Josiah pointed out the small white house built to one side of a small pond. "Thank you for letting us build the house."

"You're welcome." Delaney reached out to squeeze his hand quickly, before his father noticed. "I never planned to return, so it made sense to let you make the property your own."

Simon raised an eyebrow. "So, you agree to the terms?"

"I haven't decided." She looked over the rows of corn, stretching into the distance. "You'll know by the end of the day tomorrow."

"And you, James. What do you think she should do? After all, if you are to marry, you should have a voice in this discussion."

Before James could respond, Josiah said, "I'll be right back."

James reached out to take her hand, pleased when she didn't pull back. "This is her decision. I support whatever she wants to do."

The three of them continued to walk, and James was amazed as she asked questions about the crops and livestock, and clearly knew what the answers meant. While he was always used to her sounding confident and knowledgeable in conversations, this was a side of her that he'd never seen before.

They had just looped back around to where they started when Josiah could be seen coming from behind the barn, and the head of a horse poked out as well. Delaney stopped short, her eyes widening, and whispered, "No, it can't be!"

Simon chuckled. "It can be."

Delaney's face was pure white. "May I?"

"Delaney, why do you think Josiah is bringing him out? Go, girl, go see your horse."

As James watched in shock, she dropped his hand, and darted forward like a small child with a wonderful surprise. Running to the fence, she didn't bother to look for a gate, and instead, clambered up to the top rail, throwing her leg over it. Her voice showed her wonder. "Free?"

The horse raised his enormous head, a distinctive black slash across his cheek. She said it again. "Free?"

With the second calling of his name, the horse lifted his head up, whinnied loudly, and started to run right toward her. Josiah dropped the reins so the horse could do as he wanted.

The horse ran as fast as his huge body could go, and when he got close to her, he stopped and made a sound unlike anything James had ever heard from his mother's horses. Later, he would tell his mother it was as if the horse called out with joy. The horse then raised its head and rubbed it against Delaney's face, which was covered in her streaming tears. She reached out, balanced on the fence, to wrap her arms around his neck, sobbing as she talked to the horse, and the horse uttered back at her.

James looked at Simon in confusion. The older man shrugged. "When she was little, all she wanted was a horse. Not a pretty little fancy horse, one of these Percherons. Her father wouldn't let her have one." He shook his head. "No matter how much I try to be charitable about God's creations, that man was pure evil. And all that child wanted was a horse. She worked that farm like an adult, did everything she was asked, a good girl through and through. Anything her brother wanted? He got. Her? She got beatings. He did too, but not like her. So many bruises, so many times you could see her in pain, and no matter how many times someone tried to get the state to do something, nothing happened."

He pulled himself back from the awful memories. "One day, when she was about seven, my mare gave birth to this little runt with strange markings, and it was clear that he wouldn't survive. We did the best we could but assumed we would lose him in the cold that night. It would be the Lord's decision if it lived or died. That night, Del took off from home again, probably trying to lure her father away from her mother and brother, and the next morning, my wife found her in the barn, holding that little foal in her arms, sound asleep. She had hidden in the barn like she often did, and she saw this little needy creature and cared for him. He survived, and I had my wife go make an agreement with her mother that as long as she came and cared for him, he was her horse, and her father never knew a thing about it. Every single day, except for some when she was in the state's care and was too far away to walk here, she came, and took care of him better than my own children cared for our livestock. And the horse? Freedom, she called him. He loved her like nothing I've ever seen." He looked down. "When her chores were done, she would come, put a bridle on him, and ride him bareback like the wind." Emotion choked his voice. "When she was with that horse, it was the only time she looked like a child."

James looked over and saw that Delaney had hopped down from the fence, and was leaning against the huge draft horse, who towered over her. He could see that she was saying something to Josiah, who nodded, then handed her the reins. With a smile, he gave her a boost onto the horse's back, and then turned to open the gate.

Slowly, Delaney walked the horse through the gate, muscle memory kicking in. How many years had it been since she'd been on a horse? Since the night before she left for college when she had ridden Freedom through most of the night.

She stopped beside James and Simon. "Simon, may I?"

"Child, he is your horse. We've kept him exercised, but he has always waited for you. Go! Ride. We are going in for some of Salom's pie."

Delaney looked at James. "Okay?"

"I'm getting pie—go!"

With a grin of pure joy, Delaney put her heel to the horse's side, and started at a slow jog down the road that led further into the farmland. Within seconds, the horse was picking up speed, and the last James saw, they were galloping across a pasture. He looked at the two men. "Thank you."

"Nothing to thank us for. We knew she would return some day, and he's her horse."

An hour later, after a slice of amazing apple pie, James thanked Simon's wife for her hospitality. Walking back outside to the wide front porch, he could see her leading the horse back, talking to him, as much at peace as he'd ever seen her.

After caring for the horse, Delaney came over to the porch. Sitting in one of the rocking chairs, she looked at the two farmers. "I can't thank you enough for caring for Freedom. I…" Her voice cracked. "I couldn't bear to ask what happened to him, and to see him, ride him again, means more than I can tell you."

Simon rocked. "He's your horse. Always will be. As long as he lives, we will care for him, and after he passes, you always will have one of his line if you want."

"Thank you." She swallowed. "Simon, Josiah, I accept your offer. The farm is yours."

James was surprised that she would announce her decision without talking to Jesse first, but seeing the look of peace on her face, he knew she'd made the decision for the right reasons.

Chapter Forty-one

Less than twenty minutes later, they were back in the car, James driving, headed to the infamous restaurant. They rode in silence for a while, then she said, "Thank you for supporting me on selling the farm."

He took a quick look at her before turning his attention back to the unfamiliar road. "Love, that was your decision. If you'd wanted to keep it, or even move here to live on it, we would've figured it out." He smiled as he glanced at her again. "But I have to tell you, when you made the decision, you looked more at peace than I've seen you in a while."

"It was the right time to make that decision." Her voice trembled. "And to see Free, to ride him. That was more than I could ever have expected. I thought he had died a long time ago."

"Simon said the only time he saw you look like a child was when you rode." He shook his head. "Watching you ride away on him, you looked so tiny. I can't even fathom what it must have looked like when you rode him when you were a kid."

"He was my best friend then. When I'd go see him, everything was okay." Delaney was looking out the window, and her voice was cautious. "What did you mean that all law students learn about the case?"

His eyes widened, thinking that she had stopped thinking about the conversation on the plane, and he tried to think how to word his answer. "It gets brought up in ethics classes, in terms of the number of times people tried to report what was going on, and yet due to your dad's power, no one did anything. Then, once your parents were dead, and you inherited everything, the executor of the estate tried to fleece you as I'm sure you knew, leading to laws about double sets of executors in situations like this. Then, there was the issue of the life insurance, as your brother was a rider on your mother's policy, and so the insurance company paid out for him, but tried to refuse to pay for your unborn sister."

"Oh."

For the rest of the drive she was silent, other than giving him directions. When they came to what was obviously the main street of the little town, he smiled seeing the big "Del's" sign on a diner at the end of a block. He chuckled. "I assume that's where we're going?"

She sighed. "Yup."

Getting out of the car, she looked up at the familiar sign. "My mom was so proud when she opened this restaurant. The idea was it would be ours, and that Jacob and my dad would have the car dealerships." She shook her head. "Time to get on with it."

At the top step, she hesitated for a moment, then took a deep breath. Pulling open the door, she shouted, "Hello? Hello, I'm Delaney. Jeanine sent me to cook today." There was no answer so she repeated, "Hello!"

"Hold on. I'm coming," sounded a grouchy voice, as an older black man, covered by a large apron, came out from the kitchen. His eyes widened, and he put one hand on the counter. "Mother of God. You've come home."

Delaney's eyes grew large as well in joy and shock. "Jasper! Oh my God, Jasper! You're still here!" Delaney raced forward and hugged the older man, and James realized that she was crying.

Jasper wrapped his arms around her like a child, lightly rocking her. "Shh, sweet child. No need for tears. You're home, and we're so glad to have you back." Still holding her, he shouted over his shoulder, "Mavis, get out here."

James couldn't see the figure belonging to the voice, but her irritation was clear. "I'll be right out. I need to get this going first."

"*Now*, Mavis. You want to see this."

"Old man, stop bossing me around." As she finished the words, she realized who was standing with Jasper's arm still wrapped around her. She set the bowl on the counter and rushed to them. "Sweet Jesus, the baby is back!"

The next minutes were mayhem as Jasper and his wife Mavis greeted Delaney and were introduced to James.

Jasper looked down at Delaney with amusement. "You know it's Monday."

She rolled her eyes. "Yes, I know it's Monday, and I know what the damn special is, and I know that I have to make it, okay?"

His grin was wide. "You still remember how?"

"How the fuck—" She looked at Mavis and blushed. "Sorry, Mavis. How the heck could I forget? Remember the month I got to make it every day?"

"Uh huh." Jasper motioned to the kitchen. "Let's go."

Mavis put a hand on James' arm. "Do you know the meatloaf story?"

"Just that she hates it."

She pulled him over to the cash register where there was a framed picture of a spray painting on the sidewall of the diner that said "*J. is a BITCH!!!!!!!*"

James looked at Mavis in confusion. "And?"

She shrugged. "Del hated making meatloaf. When she was sixteen, she refused to make it anymore. So, Jeanine told her she either made the meatloaf, or she was grounded for one week for every time she refused. She refused, got grounded, couldn't go to the fair with her cousin, and so she snuck back here, and spray painted the diner. Jeanine grounded her for a month, and also made meatloaf the special every day for a month, and she had to make it…"

James started to laugh. "That's awesome."

She gave his hand a squeeze. "That girl of yours has the heart of a lion, stronger than anyone you will ever know—except Jeanine—and loyal as the day is long. But she also has a fragile side, easily hurt." She patted his face. "She loves you. It comes off her in waves."

"Thank you. And I love her just as much."

"I know." She pointed to the kitchen. "Come on, let's put you to work."

Two hours later, the diner was full to capacity, and James watched in amazement as Mavis handled all the tables, while Jasper and Delaney cooked, arguing the whole time. James got appointed to run the cash register and bus tables.

As new customers arrived, and realized Delaney was there, she was called out from the kitchen over and over and welcomed back with open arms.

Finally, the last customer paid his bill, and as he walked out the door, Mavis yelled, "Done!" and flipped the sign on the door to "Closed."

Delaney walked out of the kitchen, her cheeks flushed, her curls wilder than normal. "Thank God!" She poured herself some water and sat at one of the stools at the counter.

Jasper came out, got himself a cup of coffee, and looked at her. "You did good, Del. It was like you never left." He nodded at James. "And you. You did good for a rookie."

James felt irrationally proud. "Thanks!"

Mavis chuckled. "Never had someone working the register as good looking as you."

"Thanks!"

Jasper looked at Delaney fondly. "Okay, little girl. One time offer. Since you had to make the meatloaf, we'll finish cleaning up. You and James get out of here. We'll see you tomorrow, unless you're too worn out, then just call, and we'll make it work somehow."

Delaney looked at him seriously. "I know I should argue with you, but I want a shower so badly it hurts, so yes, we'll take you up on that offer."

With hugs all around, James and Delaney left the diner. At the car, Delaney looked at James, her exhaustion showing. "Do you mind driving?"

"Not at all."

In the car, Delaney buckled herself in, and said, "When you pull out, turn left onto Highway 12. Stay on the highway for a while."

He was surprised. "We aren't going to the hospital or hotel?"

She shook her head, her eyes closed. "No. I talked to Jeanine about an hour ago. She sounded good and said for us to take a break this afternoon. I told her we'd be there in the morning." She paused and opened her eyes to look directly at him. "And I want to show you something. That's why we aren't going to the hotel."

"Okay." He put on the blinker. "Then let's go."

The drive took almost forty minutes, taking them farther from Fort Wayne and into a more rural and less populated area. James noticed with interest that Delaney was clearly getting more excited as the drive progressed, and by the time she said, "Turn left onto that dirt road Number Nine," she was almost wiggling in her seat.

James drove carefully down the dirt road. Suddenly, through the trees, he could see water shimmering. The road ended with a small parking area, near a beautiful timber house, with a huge porch looking out at a glassy, still lake. He stopped the car and turned off the engine.

Delaney almost jumped out. "Come on!"

James got out of the car, seeing her waiting impatiently at the bottom of a walkway that led to the house. "I'm coming!"

When he reached her, she took his hand and pulled him forward. With almost childlike glee, she opened the side door and pulled him inside.

The house was gorgeous. Beautiful lines, old weathered antiques, and soft colors. It was comfortable and welcoming. Delaney looked at his face, gauging his reaction. "Do you like it?"

"It's beautiful, Laney." He focused on her, seeing the sparkle in her eyes. "Who owns it?"

"I do." She looked down at her feet, suddenly nervous. "This is the lake house I mentioned to you. It was my grandparents' place, and my dad hated it here, so I only ever came with them or my mom. It was always my favorite place." She bit her lip. "Do you really like it?"

"I love it."

She hugged him, and James felt relief flow through him at her initiating the contact. "I'm so glad." She stepped back. "If it's okay with you, I thought we could stay here instead of the hotel."

"That would be great." He looked down at his rumpled jeans and t-shirt. "Don't we need to get our stuff?"

She looked pleased with herself. "It's all here."

"How?"

She shrugged. "Anna takes care of the place for me. I pay her to keep it up for when I rent it out. So, when I had this idea, I called her and asked her to go get our stuff, pick up some supplies for us, and bring it all here."

"Aren't you full of surprises?"

Her bossy tone was back. "You go take a shower, I'll start dinner, and then I'll shower. Okay?"

"I can start dinner."

"No, I want to." She opened her arms wide. "Look around, explore. Our stuff is in the back bedroom, and there's an attached bath. Then there'll still be light if you want to go sit on the deck and sketch while I shower."

Her thought that he might want to sketch touched him. "That sounds great."

As he turned to walk toward the bedroom, he heard her take a deep breath. "James?"

"Yes?"

"I'm really glad you came to Indiana with me."

He smiled at her. "Me too."

While he showered, Delaney worked like a maniac setting the table for dinner. She put the roast and vegetables in the oven, thankful to Anna for her attention to detail. She opened a bottle of wine to breathe and put it on the counter by two glasses.

When she heard the bathroom door open, she called out, "Want a beer on the deck?"

He came to the bedroom door dressed only in his pants, rubbing the dark hair of his broad chest with a towel. "That'd be perfect."

Two minutes later, he came into the kitchen, and Delaney handed him a beer. He smiled down at her. "Thanks, love."

"You're welcome." She wrinkled her nose. "Now, if you'll excuse me, I need a shower. I smell like friggin' meatloaf."

His grin was playful. "I like meatloaf."

She rolled her eyes. "You and everyone else, I'm told." She gestured toward the lake. "Take your beer, go look around, I'll be out in a few."

"I will." As she turned to walk away, he needed to ask the question that had been foremost on his mind all day. "Laney?"

"Yes?"

"Are we okay or...*will* we be okay?"

She turned and slowly walked toward him, stretching up on her tiptoes to place a chaste kiss on his lips, the first time she had kissed him in days. Pulling back, she looked up at him, and whispered, "We will be okay."

In the shower, Delaney washed her hair twice, needing to make sure that all hint of meatloaf was gone. Stepping out, she dried off quickly, slipping into leggings and a soft t-shirt, foregoing any underwear or bra. Barefoot, she walked soundlessly back to the kitchen, and saw James out on the deck, sketch book in hand, as he worked on something intently.

As the door was open, Delaney could step out onto the deck without him knowing it. She stopped as she realized that he was sketching Freedom, and she felt her heart catch with emotion. Without making a sound, she turned and slipped back into the house.

In the kitchen, Delaney shouted, "I'm just checking on dinner, then I'll be out."

"Need help?" She could tell he was distracted by his sketch.

"All set, thanks."

Quietly, she pulled out the ice bucket, filled it with ice, and slipped the bottle of champagne out from where it had been hidden in the produce drawer. She tucked the bottle under her arm, grabbed two glasses, and took it all to the dining room.

Working carefully, she arranged it all on the table, pulling out the note she had written earlier that day, and leaning it up against the ice bucket.

Her heart racing, Delaney almost tiptoed back to the kitchen. She took a quick look at the dinner, then stepped back out on the deck. "Almost ready."

"Great." He looked up and over his shoulder. "You made meatloaf for dinner, right?"

She rolled her eyes. "Very funny." She came near to look over his shoulder. "What are you drawing?"

He looked down, changing the shading on one line of the drawing. "Something amazing I saw today." With one final tweak, he handed the sketchbook to her. "For you."

The picture was a simple line drawing of Freedom and Delaney as they had been at the fence. He had captured the emotion of the moment, and it was absolutely beautiful. "Thank you." She put a hand on his shoulder to squeeze it gently. "I love it." She touched the horse's face reverently. "When we get home, I want to get it framed, if that's okay with you."

He was thrilled by her reaction. "Absolutely."

Delaney put the sketchbook down on the little table, walking around to stand in front of James. She felt more nervous than she had on their first date. She looked at him seriously. "Hi."

"Hi." He could see the streaks of color on her cheeks. "You okay?"

She smiled broadly. "I am. I'm more than okay."

He gestured to his lap. "Would you like to sit with me?" He pointed to the bottle on the little table. "I'll even share my beer with you."

"You'd share with me? Since when?"

He picked up the bottle and held it out to her. "Since I'm trying so hard to woo you, that's when."

She took a swig, then moved to sit on his lap, snuggling into the warmth of his embrace. Handing him the bottle, she put a hand on either side of his face and leaned in so that her forehead touched his. "You don't need to woo me; you already have me."

His eyes were uncertain. "You sure of that?"

"Never surer of anything." She leaned forward to kiss him, smiling as his arms clamped around her as if he'd never let go again.

It went from a gentle kiss of understanding and forgiveness, to one that deepened by the second. James tried hard to keep from pulling her closer, wanting to let her lead how far they went. When his hands moved to caress her back, his heart soared when he heard the familiar catch of her breathing. When her hands went to slide under his shirt, he felt compelled to stop. Putting a firm hand over hers, he pulled back slightly. "Laney?"

Her reddened lips were so sexy. He swallowed hard. Her voice was breathless. "Yes?"

"Baby, I know what I want, and I want you. I love you and want you. But for days, you've made it clear that you needed some space. I need to know that you know what you're doing right now." He moved his hand so he could stroke her cheek. "The idea that in a little while you might be thinking that this was a mistake, that's more than I can handle right now."

Laney gazed at the man in front of her, as if seeing his beautiful dark eyes and jet-black hair for the first time. For an instant, she remembered how she felt when she'd first seen him, the first time they'd kissed, the first time they had made love. Her voice was sure. "I know what I want. I love you and I want you." She grinned wickedly as she wiggled off his lap, holding out her hand. "I want you to make love to me, right now."

"And dinner?"

"Can wait."

James surged out of the chair, and before Delaney knew what was happening, he had swept her up in his arms. "Then let's go."

In the bedroom, the waning sunlight filtered in through the sheer shades. Setting her down on the bed, he asked, "Do you want the curtains closed?"

"No." As she said this, she moved so that she was kneeling on the bed, and she started to pull up her shirt.

He put his hands over hers. "No way. I get to do that."

"Oh." Delaney welcomed the familiar heat that filled her. It was so good to be back with him like this! How she had missed their physical intimacy!

He stood, feeling the wave of love as he looked at her waiting for him. She gazed up. "Remember the first time?"

Still standing beside the bed, he reached out to stroke the side of her face, seeing her body respond to his touch. "Which first time? The first time I saw you, and wanted to spend time with you, and you walked away without a backward glance?"

"It wasn't because I wasn't interested! Pam had first dibs."

He smiled, knowing the answer. "And that didn't bother you?"

"You know it did!" She smiled. "But, no, not that first time?"

"The first time we went out, and you refused to let me buy you coffee? That first time?"

"No, not that first time."

He was enjoying this game. "The first time we kissed. Let me rephrase that, when you kissed me first? After you let another woman hit on me?"

"I did not! I just…" She realized he was trying not to laugh. "No, not that first time."

"Ah." He stepped closer, putting two firm hands on her waist. "The first time we made love?"

"*That* first time."

"Yes, I remember that first time."

She pulled him close, reaching to start pushing his pants down over his thighs. "Do you remember when I told you what I needed?"

He pulled the shirt up over her head, tossing it to the side before sliding her leggings down. He was smiling as she moved to lie down so he could remove them fully as he stepped out of his pants and cast his shirt off as well. "I do." He laid down next to her, seeing her body already straining towards him. "You told me that you needed me, hard and fast, that we had the rest of our lives for slow and sweet." He moved slowly, so that his body covered hers, feeling her legs spread for him. He paused to kiss her lips before entering her. "And why do you want me to remember exactly that right now?"

She reached up, her hands clasping his backside, her body aching for him to fill her. "Because that's what I want right now. I need you like that, hard and fast, please." He started to enter her, amazed anew at how ready she was for him. "Please, James." She looked up at him, her eyes glowing. "I love you. I need you. Please make me yours again."

He tried to hold back his reaction to her words, slowly entering her while seeing her eyes darken more. He pulled back again. "You always were mine, always will be." He continued his tortuous movement, knowing he was making her crazy with frustration.

"James!"

"You don't like this?"

She sighed with pleasure as he entered her again. "You know I do, but you also know what I want…"

"I do." He leaned down and kissed her. "And I'm enjoying making you wait, at least a little bit."

With him fully inside her, Delaney tried to have a coherent thought, but all she could think of was how incredibly good he felt, and how much she had missed this over the last days. She squirmed, wanting him even more fully. "Damn you, you know what you do to me."

"And you know what you do to me." He braced himself. "Wrap your legs around me, Laney." When she hesitated for a moment he urged, "Now."

As she did what he ordered, he leaned down one more time and kissed her. "Enough waiting."

He surged into her over and over, hearing her breathing change as she came closer to her release, and feeling his own approaching rapidly. He held onto his control just long enough to hear her cry out, then spasm around him as he found his own.

Long minutes later, he pulled her into his arms. "And yes, we do have the rest of our lives for slow and sweet, and yes, I needed that too."

She braced herself on her elbow. "And yet you made me beg for it?"

He reached out to lightly pinch one nipple, seeing it immediately harden with his touch. "We both know that wasn't begging." He pinched the other. "Happy to make you beg later if you want."

She laughed. "We'll see, maybe it's my turn to make you beg…" She rubbed her finger across his bottom lip. "I missed you so much. Thank you for being patient."

"Love, you're my world. I was the one who fucked up, not you. And you were in the middle, still are, of a really weird situation. I get it, and I wasn't being patient, I was just thankful you didn't send me packing."

"I couldn't send you packing, I love you too much." She stretched. "Let's eat."

Pulling on their clothes again, they walked hand in hand to the kitchen. James poured them each a glass of wine while Delaney served two plates of dinner. As he started toward the dining area, he turned. "Do you need me to get anything? I can put this down and come back."

Delaney held back just a split second. "No, you go on in. I'll be right there." For that millisecond, she stood in doubt. What if he didn't still want to marry her? He hadn't mentioned it other than the one time at the farm. Even after they'd made love, he didn't mention it.

Picking up the plates, she walked toward the dining room, hoping she'd read his intentions correctly.

James was seated at the table, two glasses of wine next to him, as if he'd put them down quickly. Her note was in his hands, open, and she could see him staring at the words. What if she'd been wrong? Dread filled Delaney, and she turned to run.

His voice caught her. "Don't even think about it."

"About what?"

"About running." He stood up, putting the note on the table, and walking toward her slowly, his eyes unreadable. "I'll take those." James took the plates and put them on the table, then turned back toward Delaney.

In delight, Delaney watched James go down onto one knee in front of her, looking up at her in absolute love. "You had to ask if I would marry you?" He took her hands. "Delaney, would you please, please, please marry me?"

Later, Delaney would realize that as he'd knelt in front of her, tears had started to stream down her cheeks, but at that moment, all she could do was fall into his arms. "Yes! Please!"

Long, kiss-filled moments later, James pulled back, standing, and pulling her to her feet. "Come sit down and eat. Then we can plan."

As he helped her into her chair, he looked at her, his eyes sparkling. "So once again, you knew something before I did. First it was spending the night, then you clearly had this all planned if you had champagne here and everything, and again, I was the last to know." He leaned down, his lips almost brushing hers. "I'm so going to make you beg…"

"Bring it on."

After dinner, James carried the dishes into the kitchen. "I've got these. Do you want to go sit on the deck with our champagne or is it too chilly?"

"Let's sit outside. We can bring a blanket."

"Then you bring stuff out, I'll clean up and meet you out there."

Delaney walked back to their bedroom, grabbing a sweatshirt and a quilt. "Do you want a sweatshirt?"

"Please. Just bring it out on the deck."

As the sun set over the lake, taking its heat along with it, the temperature was beginning to drop. Delaney spread the huge quilt over the chair, knowing that they would sit together, and that way, they could wrap it around themselves. She put the two glasses on the little table next to the ice bucket, then went to stand looking out at the lake. How she loved this view! How many times had she stood here with her mom or grandparents and actually relaxed for a bit? It suddenly hit her—this was one of the few places she'd felt safe before her father died. No wonder she'd wanted to bring James here. Maybe they could come here sometimes, maybe...

She didn't realize that James had come up behind her, but she suddenly felt the warmth of his body as he came close. Wrapping his arms around her from behind—like he had done so many times before—he smiled as she leaned back against him. He kissed her temple. "Where are you?"

"Looking at the lake." She smiled and squeezed his arms. "I suddenly realized that I always felt safe and loved here. That's why I wanted to come here with you. I wanted to share it with you."

"Thank you." He nuzzled her neck. "So, there is another matter we need to settle."

She was baffled. "There is?" She turned around in his arms, so she could look up at him.

He grinned. "There is." He reached in his pocket. "There is the matter of your engagement ring."

James let go of her to pull the small box out, and then opened it. Delaney stared in wonder at the absolutely gorgeous diamond solitaire glowing in the twilight. Her voice cracked when she said, "It's beautiful. Oh, James…" She looked up at him like a delighted child. "Is it really for me?"

He laughed. "Yes, Delaney, it's for you." Taking it from the box, he slid it on her finger, "I bought it weeks ago, and have been dying to give it to you."

She held her hand up to catch the fading sunlight. She looked at James as a smile was spreading across her face. "I can't wait to be your wife."

Epilogue

James stood at the center table in his studio, and at hearing Delaney's soft breathing, he pulled a leather-bound sketch book out of the drawer where it had been hidden. Now that she was asleep, he could finish his gift for her in anticipation of their first wedding anniversary the next day.

Flipping through the pages was like a walk down memory lane of their year together. There was the drawing of her hand with her engagement ring, the day after he'd given it to her, as she'd held Jeanine's hand while she slept. There was the drawing of Delaney, Jasper and Mavis hugging on the day that she'd gifted them her half of the restaurant. The sketch of the first time they'd caught Jeanine and Luther holding hands last Thanksgiving. The sketch of Delaney hugging Devon when they'd asked him to be the ring bearer for their wedding. Another of Delaney's bare feet peeking out from under her wedding dress when she took off her heels to dance the bunny-hop with the children. Then their first Christmas tree. A sketch of the view from their deck on the beach in Thailand for their belated honeymoon. A drawing of Delaney, Jeanine, Luther, Jesse, Anna and their girls, all sitting on the dock watching the fireworks. His mom and Delaney brushing Freedom. His dad and Delaney in waders in a stream near the lake house. Delaney leading her first meeting as the head of the Del Foundation. The first ultrasound.

As she slept, he finished his last sketch, one of her asleep on the couch, her arms cradling and protecting their unborn child. Finishing the drawing, he took the ribbon hidden in the drawer, and tied the book with a bow. It was ready for their anniversary.

Just then he heard a noise. Delaney moved on the couch, trying to stretch her back. James chuckled. "I know someone who could help you be more comfortable right now."

Standing up, she paused for a moment, letting her body find its balance. "Until your son or daughter makes an appearance, I don't think I'll be comfortable. The little darling has a foot shoved in my ribcage."

James stood up, walking behind his very pregnant wife, wrapping his hands around their child. With a gentle nudge, he helped reposition the baby, and smiled as he heard her sigh of pleasure. "I stand corrected. That helped a lot. Thank you."

He kissed her temple. "You're welcome."

James came into the kitchen, seeing Delaney pacing slowly. "So, why don't you just admit it?"

Stopping to hold onto the counter for a moment, Delaney grimaced. "Fine, Mister Smarty-Pants, I think I'm in labor."

"I know. The stuff is in the car. Do you want to call people, or do you want me to do it?"

Delaney paused. "Do you think anyone would be mad it we just waited until the baby was born, so…"

He came forward, wrapping his arms around his wife. "So, we get a little time with our child before the hordes descend?"

Relief flowed through her. "Yes."

"I think that's a great idea." He kissed her forehead. "Delaney McDaniels, I love you more than I can tell you. Let's go meet our baby."

Twelve hours later, James laid next to Delaney, holding his wife in one arm, the other draped protectively over their son snuggled on his bare chest. Delaney held the boy's hand, entranced by the baby. She whispered, "He's so beautiful."

"Of course he is." He kissed the baby's head. "Adam Jacob McDaniels, you are loved more than we can tell you." He chuckled. "Wow, sweetheart, thank you for such a great anniversary and Thanksgiving gift."

"My pleasure." She smiled tiredly. "Thank you."

A nurse poked her head around the door. "Laney, James, you have visitors if you're ready."

James nodded, then carefully handed his son to the nurse so he could straighten his shirt. Smiling at Delaney, he asked, "Mommy, do you want to hold Adam, or do you want me to?"

She reached out her hand, squeezing his. "You can. The grandparents are going to want to hold him too."

Luther and Jeanine were the first through the door, Luther wiping tears as he came forward. "Congratulations Lulu, James!"

Delaney motioned to the little couch. "Sit down, so you can hold him."

They sat, and James gently placed the baby in Jeanine's arms. Her voice was soft as she looked down at him. "Nana is going to read you so many books, little boy." She kissed the top of his head, covered by a knitted hat. "And I love you."

She passed the baby to Luther, who gazed at him in wonder. "And Pop-pop is going to take you to the Sox, and the ballet if you want."

Within minutes, Gail and Robert, and all the brothers and wives—including a very pregnant Pam—came in for a short visit. The baby was passed between loving arms until James realized that Delaney was tiring.

With kisses good-bye, the family left, and Delaney snuggled thankfully into her husband's arms, their son cuddled between them. As her eyes started to close, James whispered, "Happy anniversary and happy Thanksgiving, love. There is nothing on earth I'm more thankful for than the two of you."

Acknowledgements

Many people and organizations helped to make this book possible. I'd like to thank Between the Lines Publishing for their belief in this project. Thanks for Misty for her incredible editing, and to Cyn for her amazing editing in earlier drafts.

Thanks to Ben, Linnea, Shane, Ryan and Amy for their excitement about every one of my writing projects, and for their constant love and support. Thanks to Ed for showing us around Indiana, and for always being there for us, and for helping me keep the memory of Annabelle Rose alive for generations to come.

Kris Francoeur, writer and educator holds Master's degrees in both Counseling Psychology and Educational Leadership. Kris has published four books: *More Than I Can Say*, *That One Small Omission* and *The Phone Call* using her pen name Anna Belle Rose, as well a memoir about grief entitled *Of Grief, Garlic and Gratitude*. Kris lives in beautiful Addison County, Vermont with her husband and youngest son, an alpaca, sheep and chickens, and usually can be found either at her spinning wheel or in her gardens.